WAPKE

INDIGENOUS SCIENCE FICTION STORIES

WAPKE

INDIGENOUS SCIENCE FICTION STORIES

Marie-Andrée Gill ~ Katie Bacon ~ Louis-Karl Picard-Sioui
Virginia Pésémapéo Bordeleau ~ Michel Jean ~ Jean Sioui ~ Cyndy Wylde
Elisapie Isaac ~ Isabelle Picard ~ J. D. Kurtness ~ Natasha Kanapé Fontaine
Janis Ottawa ~ Alyssa Jérôme ~ Joséphine Bacon

SELECTED BY

Michel Jean

TRANSLATED BY

Kathryn Gabinet-Kroo

EXILE
editions

singular fiction, poetry, nonfiction, translation, drama, and graphic books

Library and Archives Canada Cataloguing in Publication

Title: Wapke : Indigenous science fiction stories / selected by Michel Jean ;
    translated by Kathryn Gabinet-Kroo.
Other titles: Wapke. English.
Names: Jean, Michel, 1960- editor. | Gabinet-Kroo, Kathryn, 1953- translator.
Description: Translation of: Wapke. | Stories by: Marie-Andrée Gill, Katie Bacon,
    Louis-Karl Picard-Sioui, Virginia Pésémapéo Bordeleau, Michel Jean, Jean Sioui,
    Cyndy Wylde, Elisapie Isaac, Isabelle Picard, J.D. Kurtness, Natasha Kanapé
Fontaine, Janis Ottawa, Alyssa Jérôme, Joséphine Bacon.
Identifiers: Canadiana (print) 20220407134 | Canadiana (ebook) 20220407363 |
    ISBN 9781550969948 (softcover) | ISBN 9781990773006 (EPUB) |
    ISBN 9781990773013 (Kindle) | ISBN 9781990773020 (PDF)
Subjects: CSH: Science fiction, Indigenous (French) — Québec (Province) —
    Translations into English. | CSH: Indigenous fiction (French) — Québec
    (Province) — Translations into English. | CSH: Indigenous fiction (French) —
    21st century — Translations into English. | LCGFT: Science fiction. | LCGFT:
    Dystopian fiction. | LCGFT: Literature. | LCGFT: Short stories.
Classification: LCC PS8329.5.Q8 W3713 2022 | DDC C843/.087620806 — dc23

Original title: Wapke, copyright © 2021 Les Éditions Stanké, Groupe Librex inc.,
Une société de Québecor Média, Montréal (Québec) – All rights reserved
Translation copyright © Kathryn Gabinet-Kroo, 2022
Cover and pages designed by Michael Callaghan/cover art by agsandrew
Typeset in Fairfield and Plantagenet Cherokee fonts at Moons of Jupiter Studios
Published by Exile Editions Ltd ~ www.ExileEditions.com
144483 Southgate Road 14 – GD, Holstein, Ontario, N0G 2A0
Printed and bound in Canada by Imprimerie Gauvin

Conseil des Arts   Canada Council
du Canada   for the Arts   Canada   ONTARIO CREATES

We gratefully acknowledge the financial support of the Canada Council for the Arts,
the Government of Canada, and Ontario Creates toward our publishing activities.

Canadian sales representation:
The Canadian Manda Group,
664 Annette Street, Toronto ON M6S 2C8.
www.mandagroup.com 416 516 0911

North American and international
distribution, and U.S. sales:
Independent Publishers Group,
814 North Franklin Street,
Chicago IL 60610 www.ipgbook.com
toll free: 1 800 888 4741

FSC MIX Paper FSC® C100212

TEN DAYS ON BIRCHBARK

Marie-Andrée Gill

Day 1

I'm taking up writing because I broke my leg. Neka gave me a pencil that I sharpened with my knife. I've gotten pretty good at sharpening my knife; it's never cut so well. My brother went to get me a whole bunch of bark to use as paper. I can't do very much because I have to stay sitting or lying down while the others go about their business as usual. At first, I didn't feel like writing, but now time seems to drag on. My hand goes numb quickly; it's been a long time since I held a pencil. The last time was at school, I think.

I don't know what to write about so I'll talk about school. Before, we lived in our community. I had a hard time getting up in the morning. It was hard to get up and spend the whole day sitting in front of my computer, learning about stuff that bored me. For a while, I was happy not to have school anymore. But then later, from time to time, I missed it. I also missed playing online with my friends, taking a hot shower, ordering food in. Pizza, poutine, French fries, soda pop. Just writing those words make my mouth water. Words are powerful, in any case. But now, I think less and less about such things. I've gotten used to it. Here at the camp, I get up every morning because everyone has a job so we can make sure we're not missing anything. We really have to work together because we never know if we'll have enough game-meat or fish. Can't mess around with that, is what my mother says.

Day 2

My leg hurts. It throbs. *N'tuss* made me a kind of cast with a piece of wood and some fabric. I'm already up, before the others, but I can't do anything useful so I take my pieces of bark out and write on them. *N'tuss* made me a big pot of tisane with a plant that helps get rid of pain, something like Tylenol, she said. I do what Neka does in the morning, and I turn the knob on the radio. I scroll through the whole line of stations, but I get static on every one. I shut it off right away to go easy on the batteries. We save them like crazy. We have only two packs left after this. Jack is good at organizing the stuff we have left, but he still gets on my nerves sometimes.

About a month ago on the AM band, we heard people speaking with an Atikamekw accent. We hadn't heard strangers' voices in a long time. When we were first here, even though the cellular network hadn't worked in a while, we sometimes heard people on the radio. But it's been a few months now since that stopped happening. Anyhow, right now, I remember being really ticked off to learn that somewhere out there lived other people who had managed to tinker together a radio. I was happy for them but also a little jealous. We don't have anything we could use to make a radio, and even less knowledge about how to go about it. Too bad that *Mushum*, my grandfather, died not long after we settled here. At least he knew about electronics. He'd once told me that he'd been the first in the community to make a TV antenna and that he could get programs that no one else could see. I was younger then, and I wasn't too interested in all that so I listened with only half an ear. I spent most of my time playing my games, trying to reach Tops 1 and to improve my level. When I think back on it, yes, I had fun, but it no longer means anything. I played because I didn't have anything else to do. One time, my mother took away my console for a few days because I'd said some bad things to her. I was very, very fru ~~and I'd said that life wasn't worth living if she was going to take away my only pleasure. No one better read these lines, I'm embarrassed about having said that.~~

Day 3

Here, we're too busy to think. Sometimes we play cards, Cribble, or checkers, but my favourite games are Mitts, Asshole, and 945. We don't play often, especially these days, it's fall and the days are short, and it's been a pretty long time since we've had anything for light in the evening, aside from cattails dipped in grease, which don't last very long anyway. When we were at the camp at Lake Mekuau, we had propane and candles. We didn't think we were going to end up staying in the woods this long. We knew things weren't ever going to be the same as before but not that everything was completely over, that "civilization" as we had known it was gone. In the beginning, there was news on the radio that talked about the crisis, but slowly, we began to hear less and less. There was news only at noon, and it didn't last long. After that, it stopped. So we no longer knew what was happening in other places. I remember thinking it was really surreal.

Everyone is outside dealing with the female moose that Simba and I killed the other day. But I'm inside, doing little odd jobs. The sun has completely risen, and my cousin Noée is starting to have contractions. She's sitting on the chair outside; I can see and hear her. She'll be laughing and telling jokes, and then a second later her face shows that she's in pain and she breathes hard. My mother put more water on the fire, and she's boiling plants. One is Labrador tea, but I don't know what the other one is.

Day 4

At night, Noée gave birth. When it got dark, most of us sat around the fire outside to give them – Noée, my mother, my Aunt Becca, and Jason – some space. Seems it all went well, even though she looked liked she was suffering more than I had when I got my leg caught in the branch the other day. That's the second baby Noée's had since we left. I hope that this one will live. (R.I.P. Baby Pien.)

Day 5

N'tuss thinks it's funny that it was called "civilization" because in her opinion, that world was never civilized. She says that being civilized means taking care of living things. And in the world we were living in, it was just the opposite. That's why we ended up here. *N'tuss* has studied these questions a lot. She went to university. She sometimes talks about it but not that much. She's very busy all day and works hard. Most of the time when we all talk together, it's to tell stories about what happens to us here, our adventures and our misadventures. The other day, Noée's boyfriend Jason was chased by a mother bear. Nels was there too, and he said that Jason tried to get away, squealing as he ran. It's so funny when he imitates him, with the gestures and all that. It's hard to explain humour in writing. In any case, we've teased him about it ever since, until he gets fed up, and then it's even funnier.

We're like that. He'd better start getting to know us a bit. "Don't stop laughing or teasing, that's what makes us so strong," says Neka. I'm pretty sure that it's true because without it, things would be even harder. I think the hardest part is knowing that poutine and pizza were once part of my life. If I'd always lived here, I wouldn't know what I was missing.

Day 6

The baby is a girl. Her name is Uastessiu because she was born at the time when leaves fall. Since I can't move, I'm the one who rocks her. She's so tiny and cute. She has a birthmark on her cheek, near her ear, and that makes her special, as if she's going to have a superpower or something like that. I like believing in that. In superhero movies, they always seem to have something special like that on their body: different hair or eyes, a birthmark that gives them some kind of power. I hope that her main power is that she'll have a long life, and also that she'll be a good hunter because we're going to need that before long. She'd definitely be better than me, in any case. And she won't miss the life we had "before." If I have to describe the shape of her birthmark, right now from the angle I'm at, I'd say it looks like the continent of Africa.

Day 7

I have nothing to say.

There are six beds in our camp. Five bunk beds and a single bed that is also Simba's sofa. A big table. For cooking, there's a big wood stove with "Bélanger" written on it. Open cupboards. Inside, there are jars of meat, cattail hearts, Jerusalem artichokes, and blueberry jam; there's dried blueberries and mushrooms, and all kinds of other things. There're also remedies that *N'tuss* makes. And salt.

There are 12 of us:

Neka (my mom)

Nelson (my oldest brother)

Derek (my second oldest brother)

N'tuss Cindy (my mom's oldest sister)

Jack (her boyfriend, my uncle)

Kukum Denise (Jack's mom, who we call Grandmother)

Noée (my cousin, Cindy and Jack's daughter)

Jason (her boyfriend)

Uastessiu (baby girl)

Rebecca (my cousin, Cindy and Jack's daughter)

Simba (a family friend, his real name is Jacob, but no one calls him that)

And me.

Day 8

I don't know what to write. I don't like English. The only things I liked when we were in the village was playing hockey when we still could, playing my video games, and going up into the woods. These days, I like it when we have a Mitts tournament, I like rocking the baby, but I especially like it when I kill a moose (I've already killed my third, but it's a good thing I'm not all alone). The first time I fired, I missed. It was Jack who had passed me the rifle so that I could try. But after that, I got better. That was before we began to scrimp on .30/30 cartridges. Now we shoot only when we're sure we won't miss. Me, Simba, Nels, and Becca try to make bows and arrows, and practice shooting so we'll be ready when we have no more bullets. Looks like we'll have to work quite a bit harder when that happens. It was during our very first attempt at bowhunting that I broke my leg. I "called" a female, and I heard her coming. I climbed into a tree because we were out in the open, and there was just one big tree. I know, not a great idea. The female came almost right beneath the tree, and I shot one arrow and then another, but I lost my balance and when I fell, my leg stayed hooked in a fork of a branch, and I was left hanging upside down. Just remembering the scene is enough to shoot pain down my leg; I never felt such pain in all my life. I must have yelled really loudly because it wasn't long before Simba found me. He'd managed to kill the female. Lucky for that.

Day 9

I'm still totally worked up; I'm shaking. Today we met some people!!!!!!

They're going to set up their tent on the beach tonight.

Day 10

Their names are Patrice, Shiship, Mikisiw, and Morgane. They told us that there are several families together, if I understood correctly. They're at Lake Alfred, about 60 kilometres west of here, and they've been set up there since the end of the summer. They change locations often, twice a year. We saw them arriving at the end of the lake, in a little forest-green canoe. They had their stuff in it, but they also had crutches that they'd made themselves. They're too big, but Jack told me they'd shorten them. It seemed really weird that they'd have crutches with them. I didn't get it.

They hadn't hunted this far into the area yet, but that day, the fishing was good in a certain lake, and they'd decided to try that place and then go check out a few lakes further away the next day, and rebuild their camp for a few days. They saw evidence of our presence two lakes over from here, and they kept going in order to find us.

We wanted to ask them questions, but we too were a little embarrassed. It's so bizarre, seeing new people. It's like the words got stuck in your throat because your heart was beating too hard. I think they felt the same way. They must have been used to speaking only their language amongst themselves.

But with Simba, Jack, and *Kukum* Denise, they could speak Atikamekw, and they'd understand each other super-well. As for me, I got only little bits of it, like a radio that's only half-tuned to a station.

Neka just asked if they have a radio because we'd recently heard someone speaking English with an Atikamekw accent, on station 101.9. Yes, that was them. They have a kind of solar-powered radio that they can use to send messages. They send one almost every day, sometimes in the morning, sometimes at noon or in the evening, so that they have a better chance of reaching someone. They've been in touch with two other groups since they started living in the woods, but they've met only one other family before ours, and that was last fall.

Before they left, I gathered up my courage and asked Morgane a question (because she looked to be my age, and the adults were all talking together). I asked her why they'd brought crutches in their canoe. She said that a few days ago, she'd dreamed about an injured person and had told her great-*kukum* about it. Her great-grandmother had told her to go fishing with the men and to take along the crutches that they had, just in case her dream turned out to be true.

I think this will be my last day of writing. Starting tomorrow, I can walk. And soon, I'll go visit them over there.

CÉCILE

Katia Bacon

6:00 a.m. As usual, Cécile opens her eyes, the same time every morning. She sits on her tiny bed, and at 6:05 a.m., she prays. She recites the rosary with the beads her daughter brought back from her trip to Medjugorje. One bead for the *Our Father*, three for *Hail Mary*, one *Glory be to the Father*, 10 *Hail Marys*, one *Glory be to the Father*...

6:30 a.m., Cécile has recited a total of 50 *Hail Marys*, five *Glory be to the Fathers*, and two *Our Fathers*. It's time to get dressed.

She puts on black pants, a white shirt, and a mauve vest. The vest is the only piece of clothing which changes colour as the days go by. It's a minor change for her. Next, from under her pillow, Cécile takes her immense metal cross and slips it around her neck. The cross comes from the Sainte-Anne-de-Beaupré basilica, a place that she holds especially dear. A quick comb through her silver-grey hair, and now Cécile can go eat.

The table was set the night before; a plate is set on a place mat, between the knife and the spoon. On this plate, there is a bowl. In the corner, her teacup. Another place mat in the centre of the table on which sits the box of cereal, the sugar bowl, the pint of milk, and the sweetened condensed milk that Cécile loves to put on her toast.

Although Cecile eats little, she takes a surprisingly long time to finish her breakfast. Between each mouthful, she gets lost in her memories. She replays them in her mind for fear of forgetting them. Her husband. Her children. Her grandchildren.

"I love you," she tells them, again and again.

As soon as she finishes eating, she puts everything away, washes the plates, cup, and utensils. A dishwasher was installed years ago, but it was never used. Cécile has always washed everything by hand, thus avoiding having to learn how to use it.

One day, without warning, Cécile saw her house invaded by men, all dressed in white. They were there to install a variety of equipment. They hung screens in every room. Cameras. Shelving. Food dispensers.

A woman, a translator, was there to explain things to Cécile because she doesn't speak French. "Use this to open the screen, and this is to communicate with Iris, a young relative of yours. This button is…" She stopped midsentence because she could clearly see that Cécile's mind was wandering. She didn't understand anything and didn't want to.

>~~~<

After lunch, Cécile prepares her tea. Day after day, she uses the same cup, the white one with the little crack on the side. The tea is poured until the cup is half full, and then she adds two teaspoons of sugar and lots of milk. Always.

Her cup in one hand, her cane in the other, Cécile goes to the tiny room from which she can look out the window once she is seated in the old wooden rocking chair.

Before, she could watch her neighbours. The woman on the right used to spend her time washing her car. The one on the left sold bread – Cécile could still smell its aroma. There was also Mr. Ashini, the bus driver who adored children. Unleashed dogs chased after cars. The neighbourhood was bursting with life!

But that? That was before…

Now what does she see? Grey to the left. Grey to the right. Grey straight ahead. Not a soul.

Hoping to calm an angry people, the new directors decided several years ago to forbid outings. Anyone who went outside was putting himself in danger. The frequent demonstrations, multiple bombings, and innumerable attacks eroded national security. Draconian measures were put in place to prevent any violation of this law.

The government spent thousands, if not millions of dollars to barricade each house with iron cladding equipped with an aeration and remote door-opening system. Workers managed to make the ground inaccessible by raising the dwellings. A government organization handles the distribution of supplies and provides for essential needs. Everything is monitored.

This reminds Cécile of the evening, back in the 1940s, when an important national company, under orders from the Duplessis government, flooded her family's land.

She was 10 years old when Canadian explorers appeared in the forest. Upon seeing them search everywhere and look around them with such curiosity, she told herself that the place must be of some particular interest. Cécile found them intrusive but kind.

A few weeks later, a deafening racket woke Cécile and her family during the night. They had never heard such a noise. They all left the tent to try to understand. A huge wave surged toward the encampment. It seemed as if someone was spilling an enormous bucket of water. Her father immediately began gathering things up.

"Take everything you can! Anything that we can use to reach the mountain. Food, clothing, tools, weapons!"

Wasting no time, Cécile, her mother, father, and two brothers began a long trek, leaving their submerged camp behind. It took them two days to reach high ground, where some 10 families had already gathered. All had experienced the same nightmare.

A man appeared before them, and Cécile recognized one of the explorers, one whom she had found to be friendly.

"We know that you've been deprived of the skins that sheltered you, and that's a shame. We have a solution for you. Houses, real ones, have been built so that you can stay in them all year long! We have reserved a lovely area for you where you will thrive."

The strangers took them to this promised land in a motorized vehicle with wheels. Cécile had never seen such a thing, and its noise was so thunderous that she feared an explosion. There were no roads back then, and journey seemed long and arduous. Cécile thought that walking would have been preferable. They were accustomed to travelling by foot, carrying with them all that was necessary for their survival.

Several hours later, they reached the place where the houses had been erected. It was impressive!

But how had these men been able to build so many houses in so little time? How could they have known what had happened to her people?

It had taken Cécile years to understand.

><~~><

She needs to clear her mind; her eyes fill with tears when this memory resurfaces. She realizes that she can never again return to that forest.

It's 3:00 p.m. and, as she does every day, she spends her afternoon rearranging her photographs in albums that she carefully stores inside an old blue chest. Her children once used it to play pirates.

Cécile can spend hours looking at each image, remembering every detail about the moment the picture was taken. Sometimes she laughs; other times she cries. Today, in a fairly good mood, she smiles when she comes upon her favourite picture of her husband. He poses sitting in front of the house, violin and bow in his hands.

That day, he was supposed to go perform a marriage in Schefferville. A contract that would last eight days. Just before that, he had bought himself a camera: "So that I can see what happens when I'm away," he'd joked. Cécile had never seen one and didn't know how to make it work. Her husband, always on the lookout for the latest gadgets, had given a demonstration. "Hold very still here, look into this little hole and, when I'm ready, you press this button." And that's how he became her first model, the first memory she had captured in an image.

Cécile stops her musings; she hadn't noticed the time passing. She goes to the kitchen to prepare her table for supper. It's somewhat similar to breakfast: the place setting is identical, and the meal is almost the same, except that instead of condensed milk, she puts cheese on her toast. She also omits the cereal… sleeping on a full stomach gives her nightmares.

Having eaten everything on her plate, she gets up to do the dishes, as usual. However, this differs from her morning routine in that Cécile affords herself less time to daydream during this meal because afterward, she prays. Again.

6:00 p.m. Cécile enters the little room where she once upon a time waited for her brother so that they could go to Mass together. Now, sitting in her old wooden rocking chair, she prays alone. Alone is what she has been for a long time, but it wasn't always so. Cécile and her husband had children, and they were also a foster family for three children who had come from less fortunate parents. These children then had their own children. This means that Cécile never had a minute of solitude during a large part of her life. Being surrounded by people brought her joy.

Why must she be so alone now? Why her? What has she done to make God forsake her? She, who was always faithful to Him… so many unanswered questions, but she keeps praying.

Our Father, who art in heaven,
hallowed be thy name,
thy kingdom come,
thy will be done, on earth as it is in heaven.

Her rosary in her hands, she murmurs the words with conviction. God will hear her. He will come find her as he failed to do so long ago.

Give us this day our daily bread.
And forgive us our debts,
As we forgive our debtors.

It was after her second delivery. Everything had gone well. Aside from the fact that her husband couldn't make it to the hospital, Cécile was overjoyed. Her tiny daughter was in the hands of the kind nurses. Since her first had been born in a tent in the forest with her mother and aunt in attendance, she was pleased with this new experience. Even though there had been other people in the room, Cécile could rest worry free.

A bed had been placed in each of the room's four corners. Curtains served as walls, but most of the time they were drawn back. The patients had a chair for visitors. Two windows let in the light of day. Fortunately, Cécile's bed was at the back so that she could see outside.

Lying there, she thought about first names for her daughter. Her husband wanted a son this time and had prepared a list: Paul, Joachim, Pierre, Yves, Louis...

Yet he hoped that Adèle, his mother's first name, would be saved for their next daughter. She practiced it, repeating quietly, "Adèle! Adèle, go get dressed! Adèle, don't run around the table!"

Cécile thought this name quite pretty and perfect for her new baby! She couldn't wait for her husband to arrive so that she could tell him. It was a long wait, but her happiness made her a little more patient than usual. She smiled and closed her eyes.

Cécile awoke, gripped by pain in her lower abdomen. She tried to get up but couldn't. Her heart was pounding, her vision became increasingly blurry. The other patients were sleeping; she wanted to cry out, but no sound left her mouth. Little by little, she felt her mind wandering off. She was going to faint.

At that very moment, she saw a woman that she knew. Cécile forced herself to remain conscious.

"Marie! Have you seen my husband?" Cécile asked through her tears.

Marie sat on the corner of the bed and stared at her; you could almost see the pity in her eyes. But Cécile knew full well that Marie wasn't seeing her because she was blind. She knew her; the two came from the same village. The woman was known for her blue eyes, which were covered with a thin white film. This fascinated people back home because they had never seen someone with eyes that colour. Everyone else had eyes as brown as dried caribou meat.

The woman drew near to Cécile, who was in agony.

"Don't cry!"

Hands on her still numb and swollen belly, Cécile cried; the pain was getting worse. She was afraid of dying. She was afraid of leaving her husband alone with their two children. The girls were still too young to be without their mother! Her husband couldn't take care of them; he was the one who supported the family… Cécile refused to abandon them. Not now.

"It will be all right, you'll survive. Your children will grow up, your husband will love you all your life. You will see it all.

The village will grow big, and there will be many, many people. Life will change, and you will see everything. Everything."

As she opened her eyes, Cécile noticed a young nurse checking her vital signs. Her husband was sitting on the visitor's chair, the baby in his arms. Cécile was comforted to see them, believing she'd had a nightmare. It was only when she learned of Marie's death, years later, that Cécile remembered the episode at the hospital.

"You will see everything."

This sentence echoed in her head without knowing what the woman had meant to say. To thank her for saving her life, Cécile had lit a candle at her funeral service.

And do not lead us into temptation,
But deliver us from the evil one.
Amen.

Cécile finished her private Mass.

She can't see outside, but she knows that it's dark because she is overcome with fatigue. She goes to prepare her table for the next day. A plate sitting on a place-mat, between the knife and spoon. On the plate, the bowl. In the corner, her teacup. On the other place mat, the cereal box, the sugar bowl, the pint of milk, and the sweetened condensed milk that she loves to put on her toast.

She goes to her room, sits on her bed, removes the immense metal cross from around her neck, and places it under her pillow next to the photograph of Pope John Paul II, her favourite. Her fleece pyjamas are on the bed, and she puts them on. Cécile pulls back the covers and can finally lie down.

As she does every night, Cécile reflects. She reviews the day she just lived, one day more. Exhausted, but she never complains because God will come for her at the right time.

"I am ready," she says aloud, raising her eyes heavenward.

Cécile has been ready ever since the daughter of her last grandson left to join the others. She is ready, so why is she still here?

Cécile was born in a tent, one autumn evening in 1932. She grew up with two brothers but grew old with only one. The first took his own life after their deportation; he could not adapt to their new sedentary life of confinement...

At the age of 18, Cécile's very loving parents married her to a nice boy. He was an orphan and stout-hearted. He loved her his entire life. She never misses an opportunity to thank them for having chosen such a marvellous man for her.

Together, they had 17 children: 12 girls and five boys, who then had children, and then those children also had children. Her family already counted 100 members; her three-storey house was already too small to hold them all. Almost every week, it was someone's birthday. The house was the centre of the family.

She misses all of that tremendously.

Her life had been filled with small pleasures, but she'd also known her share of misfortune. Cécile had lived through three wars. She had seen cities bombed. She had seen humans attack other humans because of the colour of their skin. She had seen corpses in the streets. She had seen people who were poor, ill, disabled, unwanted.

She had seen her village become a city. She had seen her children, grandchildren, great-grandchildren, and even *their* children grow up; she had seen them leave one by one. Some went voluntarily, others naturally.

She had seen machines talk, walk, care for, work. She had seen every technological advance.

She had seen bodies of water emptied. She had seen the seasons disappear. She had seen the sun go out. She had seen the north become the south, and the south become the north.

And even more… "I've seen everything," she thinks.

Marie's voice echoes in her head once more: "You will see everything."

Now, everything is grey, and still Cécile waits.

Stretched out in bed, she turns her head to the left and stares at the picture hanging on the wall.

"Everywhere I look, it's you that I see. I'll see you soon, God willing," she says to her black-and-white husband.

Cécile closes her eyes. Tomorrow, she'll celebrate her 182nd birthday.

THE TOMAHAWK AND THE SWORD

Louis-Karl Picard-Sioui

In the darkness of the lab, Yahndawara' rocked with a slow rhythm. To reassure herself, to allow herself to forget, if only for a moment, the emptiness eating away at her. To encapsulate each of the bereavements that had accumulated inside her as the days and years went by. The young woman knew that her consolation would be short-lived, but she took the opportunity to try to find serenity, that equilibrium she so lacked, by chanting her wish as she would a mantra: "*Ahskennon'nia iye's, ahskennon'nia iye's, ahskennon'nia iye's...*" I'm at peace, I'm at peace, she intoned. Then, in the midst of a sigh, she partially opened her swollen eyelids and saw her reflection in the window that served as a wall. Her face wrinkled up unevenly with the strain of a weary breath. Her drawn features were plagued by pain, marked by a sorrow deeper than time itself. She no longer recognized herself.

Yahndawara' took one last look at the Queen City, which spread out at her feet. From the top of the tower, everything seemed minuscule. Even at this late hour, the mega-technopolis teemed with life. Recent decades had forced the city to expand upward, but it had always had its feet in the lake, as her people had foretold when they named various locations. Toronto: "Where the tree stands in the water." Sadly, this centuries-old tree would soon fall. It would meet its end in the year 2072. Although Yahndawara' refused to be happy about it, at least she had gotten used to the idea. She knew that somewhere, in another time frame, the city had not been contaminated by the Sword's ideas. Somewhere, in the endless fields of possibilities, the tree would continue to grow and flourish. But not here. Not now. The chiselling away of its roots had become an inevitability. Her years of struggle and wandering had taught her that the most painful sacrifices were sometimes the most necessary. And besides, she was aware that this year would be the tree's last.

As she was contemplating the city, Yahndawara' noticed a multitude of flashing lights converging on her position, piercing the night. They had come for her, as she had hoped they would. For her but especially for the machine. The woman allowed herself a smile, then turned away from the window. All around her, thousands of tiny indicators blinked and glowed in the shadows. They were all components of the Strendu's electronic system, a marvel of technology whose sole purpose was to analyze the space-time currents that traversed reality.

The Strendu was an aberration. The product of an unknown civilization from a distant future. A civilization that, with the adjustments the young woman's intervention unit made to the time frame, may have been eradicated from any and all possibility of existence. No matter. A few minutes had already passed since the Strendu's usefulness had plummeted dramatically. The last time warp chosen by the Sorcerer had been borrowed by Skahndawatih – and he would not be coming back. And the Sorcerer was no more. He had been mortally wounded by their pursuers from another time. Without the Sorcerer to detect the end-point of passageways, the Strendu was virtually useless. Although the system could always locate the breaches opening in the present, it could not determine the vortex's precise point of arrival. Without a guide, the Strendu was at best an assisted-suicide aide, at worst, a weapon of universal destruction. Because in malevolent hands, the system could cause enough paradoxes and anomalies to tear the web of reality itself and break the sacred circle of existence once and for all.

Obviously, Yahndawara' could not risk such an eventuality. So, she alone had stayed behind to make sure that no one could further threaten the framework of reality. So that no one would find Skahndawatih. So that no one could thwart their plan. This was her last mission, her sole motivation. At least that's what she was trying to make herself believe. And yet the truth was simpler than that. So much simpler: Yahndawara' had had enough of running.

The young woman came from far away, in the sense of both space and time. Her city had been one of the first to fall during the invasions of the 26th century. The invader had arrived via the Great Water, splitting the earth with his cross and spreading death to the four winds. The barbarian chieftain had proclaimed that all those who would not bow down to their God would be annihilated. This is what Yahndawara' was told by her mother, who had witnessed the event. Her family had chuckled over it, unable to grasp the reality of the danger hanging over them. It was only a few seasons later when this chieftain, this Cartier, had returned to invoke his curse, that they had understood the gravity of the threat. But it was already too late.

Disease and war devastated the city and struck down her family and her clan. She was no more than 10 at the time. The survivors abandoned Stadacona and took refuge in the interior, near other nations of the confederation. After all, as they said at the time: *skawendat*. A single voice. They all spoke the same language and were but one people. As Yahndawara' and her twin brother Haronhiateka' prepared to start the portage, the Sorcerer appeared before them. He had seen them in dream. He knew of the crucial role that the twins would play in the world's preservation. Above all, he knew that the fall of the city was not in the scheme of things, that all that was the result of an experiment in a distant future, where men of faith, members of an all-powerful sect known as the Universal Sword enjoyed playing at being gods. In 2124, they had created their machine, the Strendu, to traverse and alter the past. But the experiment had gone wrong, and the machine had been sucked up by the breach that the machine itself had produced. The surface of time had been cracked. In wanting to rewrite the past, they had condemned all time frames, past, present, and future. The Sorcerer knew all this because his dreams had been revealed to him.

Since the revelation, Yahndawara' had only one goal: to discover the precise origin of the spatiotemporal fissures splintering the universe, thereby averting disaster. To put an end to the ignoble project of these men of faith. To save her people from a premature death. To give them back the destiny that had clearly been stolen from them. And she had almost succeeded. She and her companions had located the Strendu. The machine was too damaged to generate new fissures, something that the Sorcerer never would have allowed. "We cannot solve a problem with the tool that created it," he had repeated. But at least the machine could still pinpoint the sporadic pathways opening into the present.

In order to go back to the source of the problem, Yahndawara' and her allies had travelled through a myriad of eras, hunted by trackers from the future seeking their holy grail, which had been swallowed up by time. Yahndawara' believed that, should they be able to evade their pursuers, she could breathe for a moment and enjoy her interlude with Skahndawatih before their final mission in 2124. But such was not the case. Shortly after their arrival in 2072, they finally subdued the Sword trackers. But they paid a heavy price. The Sorcerer was fatally wounded. They had to start all over. Time is an injured beast that refuses to be healed. And because when it rains, it pours, they soon realized that it was too late: the Universal Sword had already been raised. And if it captured the Strendu 50 years before the machine was created, the damage would be irreversible. The stakes were high, but Yahndawara' had had enough. Enough of running away and chasing after, enough of this endless quest. Since the Sorcerer's death, Yahndawara' had thought of only one thing: destroying the Sword and the machine once and for all, thus ending this manhunt. That, and of vengeance, too.

Pschhhit!

The radio receiver interrupted the young woman's thoughts. In the lab's artificially star-studded night, a voice could be heard. A hoarse voice. A familiar voice. Her brother's voice.

"Wara'? I've been waiting for you at the extraction point for 10 minutes. There a problem?"

Yahndawara' didn't break her silence, giving herself enough time to summon up the necessary courage. She had changed the plan, and so be it. She would not be leaving. He would not see her again. It wasn't enough to simply destroy the Strendu. If her brother was to live in peace, she would have to obliterate the Sword here and now. She exhaled, stood, and picked up the device with a trembling hand.

"No. No problem," she stammered. "I release you from our burden, dear brother. Take full advantage of the time you have left."

"By *Yäatayenhtsihk*! What does that mean? Don't do it, Wara'. They'll be here any minute…"

"They're already here! Run, Teka'! One of us must survive to tell the tale."

Once again, there was only silence on the frequency. A silence as heavy as the weight of the world. A world whose entire universe was sinking into the black hole of oblivion. When the man spoke again, his voice came out in a half-whisper and was interrupted by sobs. "Yahndawara'… I… I've already lost everything… This wasn't the plan!"

Yahndawara' felt the anger rumbling in her belly. She was the last woman in her mother's lineage and thus held authority over her brother, who was a few minutes younger, but time after time, he acted stubbornly. He refused to accept her watching over him. Refused to accept that she fulfil her duty. Refused to accept the inevitable. Fury filled her being, and Yahndawara' shouted, "Haronhiateka'! Stop blubbering and save yourself! You hear me? You get on the next glider to Mexico, as planned, and you disappear. Go far, very far away. I'll take care of the rest. *Over. And. Out!*"

Without waiting for his reply, she used all her strength to hurl the radio receiver against the wall. There. No further contact. Only silence. Silence and the void.

Alone in the darkness, the young woman sat back down in the armchair. She rocked her anger. She rocked her sorrow. Her mind turned to those she had left and to the one she would be leaving. She whispered a farewell song to her brother. She hummed a verse in memory of the Sorcerer. Her breath chanted a hymn to Skahndawatih, her brave warrior swallowed up by time. Time that they had never had. And, long slow sighs later, she pulled herself together. After all, the truth was so very simple. So much simpler. All the reasons to exist, hers and those of others, all the destinies and all the origins, each one of the steps in the cosmic round-dance could be reduced to their simplest equation: ultimately, the only thing that truly mattered was that Skahndawatih accomplish his mission. Without any obstacles. Without being pursued.

Yahndawara' wondered what would happen if Skahndawatih succeeded. Or if he failed. She wondered how she would know the difference. From the corner of her eye, she saw a new indicator light flash on. It was an independent warning device, in no way connected to the Strendu. A silent alarm. Yahndawara' left her armchair and rushed toward the main terminal. The young woman closed her eyes. She let her fingers hover over the keyboard for a moment. Her index finger stopped above a button marked with a strange symbol: a primitive tomahawk. She pressed. Suspended before her, the giant screen came to life. It displayed the symbol of a tomahawk, glowing red against a field of black.

Then in a cloud of dust, the only access door to the laboratory violently opened inward. A squadron of masked men entered the room. The first wave strategically fanned out around Yahndawara'. Standing stock-still, the snipers aimed their rifles at her. The young woman did not move. Standing there, she watched the military circus. A second wave stormed into the room. Fewer in number, these men hurried over to the Strendu's interaction interfaces. Armed with scanners, they probed the system, probably to confirm its authenticity and make sure it was operational. Their smiles indicated that they were satisfied. Yahndawara' was, as well; now that the henchmen were reassured, their master would appear. She waited, but not for long. A man in a green suit joined the intervention unit. He was no longer young, but his step did not betray his age. The man was Caucasian, obviously. Tall and bald. His skin was pale, his eyes as blue as the sky. The right side of his face bore a delicately tattooed sword. A sword or a cross. Yahndawara' smiled. As she had predicted, he had come in person: General Providence, Commander in Chief of the Universal Sword.

⌁⌁

Walking nobly but in a calculated manner, the general entered the laboratory. The air was dry and dusty, but that did not overly irritate him. He quickly scanned the surroundings. The room was dark. Aside from the thousands of flashing lights flickering in the gloom, the only illumination came from the main monitor, which displayed the symbol of a tomahawk. Red against a field of black.

Providence took a few steps to admire the miracle of technology more closely. The arsenal of computers was impressive. Dozens of housings in all shapes and all sizes were stacked up in the room, as were countless monitors, holographic projectors, scanners, sensors, and consoles. He was suddenly filled with a deep sense of satisfaction. He had been waiting for this moment for so long. Decades. Providence had travelled around the world in search of his holy grail. And today, at last, the S.T.Re.N.D.U. was his. He had succeeded; he had passed the test. The general smiled. Soon he would be able to take back what belonged to him. He could correct the past. And soon, yes, soon, he would deliver this world to Our Heavenly Father. And with a heart filled with gratitude, he would wield God's Sword, strike down the infidels, and purge his realm of the falsehood and its adherents.

This was certainly a great day for the Sword and its devoted worshippers. Before him, his men were still in position. They had been well-trained. Not one of the soldiers had moved since he'd entered. A tight, precise, and brilliantly executed operation. The general was proud of his army. Several men were aiming a weapon. Criss-crossing the shadows, red laser beams were all pointing toward a single target: the young woman standing in front of the main interface. She didn't seem surprised to see him. She had recognized him. "Well," he thought, "We can skip the formalities."

"At ease!" the general commanded.

The soldiers immediately lowered their rifles but stayed in position. Providence slowly advanced toward the young woman. "Yahndawara'." The sight of her face brought a flood of feelings and memories to the old man's mind. He had already met her, briefly, decades earlier. In 2030, the year when his life had been changed forever. The pivotal year when Providence had lost the one who was the dearest to him in the world. The year when he had taken up his father's torch. At the time, the Order of the Cross, precursor of the Universal Sword, was simply a pious but small-scale organization with no dreams and no future. But in 2030, he received the necessary inspiration. And Providence had risen through the cult's ranks to finally become its supreme commander, thus transforming it forever.

By now, the Sword had hundreds of thousands of soldiers and faithful followers spread across four continents. And at the age of 63, Providence was one of the most powerful people on the planet. But while his mind had remained clear, his body had grown old. The general noted that it was quite the opposite for the woman. Yahndawara' was still just as young and fresh as she was in his memory. This wasn't really surprising because during their single encounter, she and her three acolytes had fled through a temporal fissure. And a little over 42 years later, Yahndawara' was still very attractive. Naturally, the general found her skin tone to be a little too dark, her eyes a little too slanted, her appearance too... "exotic" for his taste. But the Wendat had that youthful strength that returned to old men their thirst for life.

Providence could not help feeling a certain admiration for the squaw. True, in his eyes, she was nothing but a pagan. Yet her faith was unwavering. Her loyalty, exemplary. Her determination, like iron. How could an inferior being like Yahndawara' possess these qualities? Providence had trouble understanding. After a long moment, he decided to clear his mind of these distractions to focus on the current situation. After all, he was a pragmatic man. He broke the silence: "So this is where you're hiding the S.T.Re.N.D.U.?"

"No," replied Yahndawara', sounding mysterious.

"No? Then what's all this equipment?" the man asked, gesturing at it with his hand.

"This is 'the Strendu.' You are clearly ignorant. Quite ironic for the general of a cult claiming to have the copyright on Truth."

Providence burst out laughing. A laugh both honest and threatening. The young woman's arrogance amused him. The old man admired her audacity. He was well aware that she was trying to provoke him, but it didn't stop him from answering back. In any case, he now had all the time in the world.

"I know more about it than you think, Yahndawara'. About you and your impure superstitions."

Yahndawara' said not a word. She simply observed her enemy. Her gaze gave no hint of surprise or emotion. Providence had underestimated her. She clearly expected him to remember her. The general's smile became a grin. He had other tricks up his sleeve.

"I know," Providence went on, "that you believe that the term 'Strendu' comes from one of those stupid fantastical stories that you take for the truth. If I remember correctly, it's about a man-eating giant who was defeated by a mythical hero called Skahndawatih. Rest assured that I do appreciate the poetry and the irony of it all."

The young woman seemed somewhat shocked, but she quickly recovered. Providence savoured the moment as he awaited her reply.

"Wrong again, General. In the legend, Skahndawatih doesn't really triumph over the Strendu. It's the Strendu who begins the story, and it's the Strendu who ends it. In fact, it's the Strendu herself who names the hero Skahndawatih…"

"He-who-is-always-on-the-other-side-of-the-River," interrupted the general. "I know. Fearing that the monster would devour him, the hero ceaselessly crosses the river in his canoe, avoiding the giant who must walk on the riverbed. Now, I look forward to you telling me which 'riverbank' *your* Skahndawatih has sailed to."

This time it was Yahndawara' who burst out laughing. But the slap delivered by Providence brought her back to her senses. Blood beaded on her lips. She squinted her eyes. Providence got little satisfaction from this act, but the young woman definitely needed to be disciplined. She needed to learn respect. And the general was a master of the art.

"You want to know?" she demanded. "Let me lay it out for you: Skahndawatih has gone where you can never reach him. He has gone to erase you from the surface of time. The Sword will never fall upon Mother Earth because it will never be raised!"

Yahndawara' received another blow, this time to the abdomen. She had difficulty catching her breath. The general watched her from above, his face cold as marble. But his look was more that of a mentor than of a sadist.

"Pathetic," he declared with disdain. "Seek refuge in silence if you must. This is of absolutely no importance. Soon, our scouts will have corrected history as Our Heavenly Father so desires. The Universal Sword will have accomplished His will on earth: one Law, one Faith, one King. The primitive races, the infidels, the weak, the leftists, the sexual deviants, and all those who get in the way of the humankind's manifest destiny will be expunged from our planet!"

"You don't get it," Yahndawara' retorted in a calm but severe voice. "You should not exist. The Sword is an aberration. An error, a bug in the system of reality. As for you, General, you are a liar. I don't know what rationalization you've managed to find to justify your actions, but I remember very well what motivates you…"

Providence hit her again. His rage finally got the best of him. This idiotic woman had made him lose his temper. How dare she speak to him in that tone? This primitive, this pagan? The taste of blood filled the young woman's mouth and nose. The hot red fluid ran from the corner of her mouth, trickled down the length of her neck, and spread across her chest. The world around her became a blur. She had trouble discerning shapes. She could no longer distinguish colours: red against a field of black. Yahndawara' clung to the console behind her to keep herself from stumbling. For a moment, the general thought that the young woman was going to faint, but Yahndawara' recovered. She leaned against the adjacent wall to put some distance between herself and her tormentor. Clumsily, she slid toward the window.

"Where do you think you're going like that? My forces have surrounded the building. Almost all of our people were mobilized for this operation. The S.T.Re.N.D.U. is ours. And so are you. There's nothing you can do about it."

"I belong to the Earth and to the Circle," replied Yahndawara'. "The Strendu belongs to no one. You'll get nothing out of it. Not without a guide."

"We will find the way!" interjected the general. "Or do you actually believe that the civilization that created this machine was the slave of some crazy clairvoyant? The Sword will subdue the giant cannibal. And it will enable us to defeat Skahndawatih."

"Have you understood nothing at all, General? The Strendu has her limits. And she cannot defeat Skahndawatih. Quite the contrary. In her insolence, the giant gives him the very weapon needed to destroy her!"

"Back to those legends of the faithless? Fine, if you enjoy making up stories before going to your eternal slumber. The tomahawk. To mock Skahndawatih, the Strendu spits on the warrior's tomahawk. In doing so, she accidentally gives it the power to slice through stone. Realizing her mistake, she becomes afraid and flees. That's how the story ends, right?"

Yahndawara' smiled. A red light reflected in her eyes. The silence formed a nest in the lab. The atmosphere turned heavy, oppressive, while uncertainty wormed its way into the general's thoughts. Slowly, Providence raised his eyes toward the huge monitor hanging before him. The tomahawk. Red against a field of black. He was suddenly filled with apprehension.

"The moral of this story eludes me. Tell me what it is!" demanded the general, his voice betraying his doubts.

"General Providence, this is no fable. There is no moral to the story. Only instructions. You claim to know everything about us. Tell me, since that day, whenever a stone giant draws near, what do the Wendat people shout at to make it go away?"

"Skahndawatih is here," Providence replied, instinctively.

✐~✐

A clicking was heard in the lab. The tomahawk displayed on the monitor flashed for a few seconds, then disappeared, plunging the room into darkness. The soldiers' beams still lit the face of the young woman, who tenderly sighed as she closed her eyes. "*Eskonyen'*, Skahndawatih, I'll see you again," she said to herself in her heart of hearts. "May you find the Sorcerer sooner, this time. May you guide him to us, my love."

The laboratory floor began to vibrate and throb, creating generalized panic among the soldiers.

Then, with a powerful blast, the machine exploded, carrying off Yahndawara', Providence, the Sword's troops, and finally the entire building. More than a third of the megatechnopolis of Toronto went up in smoke brought on by the quantum force of the explosion.

The year 2072 marked the end of the System for Timebased Recognition, Navigation and Displacement in the

Universe, as well as the destruction of the armed, neo-imperialist cult know as the Universal Sword.

Elsewhere, in another place and another era, a mythical hero once again met a young Sorcerer for the first time, hoping that this time would be the right time. That together, they could mend time.

THE LUMINOSITY
OF CHILDREN

Virginia Pésémapéo Bordeleau

Women had gradually forsaken pregnancy since the Event. That was the imprecise name that the People gave it so as not to revisit this phenomenon resulting from the Others' denial of the fact that their habits had destroyed the natural world. What purpose would complaining serve since the survivors had decided to cease any and all activity whose intention was to create an expectation? In the beginning, the reproductive instinct had persisted. Fortunately, there were two midwives and a doctor in the group. Then, over time, the women decided they would no longer bear children. And the new generation's offspring were not yet mature enough to reproduce.

People were unfamiliar with these words found sprinkled throughout writings from the past: "tomorrow," "in the future," and "it will happen when." They were rooted in daily tasks; they cultivated, fished, and hunted when there was nothing left in the reserves because the cold arrived in waves but never at the same time of year. There was little snow, but vegetables couldn't be grown at that temperature. The poles had shifted a few degrees, thus transforming everything the People knew, and the best thing to do was subsist day after day, eschew expectations, and live in the present moment by preparing meals, mending clothes, or playing games invented according to the mood of the most creative among them.

At the beginning of the disaster, humans had been dispersed by natural phenomena. A vast number of people had been eliminated by volcanic eruptions, earthquakes that destroyed whole cities, and tsunamis that submerged others that had been built along the seashore. Since the rising of water levels due to glacial melting could not be stopped, wild torrents had gnawed away at shorelines and overrun riverbanks. The seabed's tectonic plates slid on top of each other, elevating the submerged portions, recreating mountain chains, and shaking continents once thought unshakable. The earth had almost rolled over on itself, like a she-bear in her den.

It had taken a long time for the survivors to recover even the slightest bit from the trauma. There was a strong resurgence of suicide among adolescents and young adults. Their entire known universe – which revolved around interactions, friendships, and virtual games – had spilled into the void. Some had gone mad and disappeared without anyone knowing where to find them. Some thought it was better that way, and besides, each person could make his own choices because there were no more laws nor any more systems obliging people to obey the rules. Even feelings became the enemy for those who had the strength to go on despite the lack of future prospects. Wracked by sorrow and despair, parents of the disappeared also took the path toward death. The men and women who had chosen life knew that they should stay together, make a tacit agreement, and help each other according to their individual expertise.

When they began to discuss the situation, as they often did in the early days, they shuddered in fear at the thought of the continents and countries that perhaps no longer existed. They were totally unaware of what remained of the universe they'd known, of all the wonderful inventions that had improved their way of life until the earth could take no more. Never would they have believed that the end would come like this, in such a spectacular way. Yet concrete signs had indicated that something wasn't working anymore, signs including worldwide pandemics, illnesses transmitted from animal to human and vice versa. And the eternal mass of glaciers that had slowly melted away. Despite the economies crippled and deaths by the millions, humans had continued to believe that the Earth had unlimited resources and thus followed the trajectory toward their own extinction.

One of the groups of survivors was from the Abitibi highlands, descendants of those called "settlers" or "colonists." The majority of them were native to the region. At first, they'd had to adjust to the fetid odour that floated in the air because, despite the immensity of the planet, cadavers both animal and human gave off a stench of decay that took a long time to dissipate. The fumes also came from the upheaval of the upturned or fissured soil. They wore cloth masks soaked in pine scent that they made by scrubbing hard at the needles and resin of this tree, which grew in abundance at the foot of the hills. The air had gradually been cleansed of the dust spewed by volcanos.

No one wondered about the pure coincidence that brought people of every colour to this place, unique in its solidity, thanks to a subsurface composed of Precambrian magma set at the foot of ancient mountains miraculously preserved from the catastrophe. Moreover, this vast region was located hundreds of metres above sea level, an altitude that had protected it from northern waters.

This multi-ethnic population was joined by a contingent that had arrived from China. This group was comprised of students who had come to take mining-exploration courses given by a new university whose mandate was to open up to the world. Then came labourers, both men and women from African countries and from Haiti, who had been hired to fill jobs in education, social work, medicine, and mining. There was even a descendant of the native peoples once known as "Australian Aboriginals." As for the professionals from the southern part of the country, they refused to leave the capitals to settle in this zone, which they considered to be austere and inhospitable.

However, the inhabitants of Abitibi welcomed others warmly, and they were endowed with a large social conscience, thanks to which they had escaped the epidemics. They did not hesitate to close their borders, and they refrained from holding gatherings that the majority of other regions could not forego, seeing this as a matter of life and death. They were fun-loving and were compared to the indomitable Gauls from a comic strip that had left its mark on history.

Explorers had travelled through the territory, hoping to find other humans or communities where they might find materials to improve their daily life. Since there was no more electricity, they had to resort to the use of rudimentary tools to topple trees to feed the fireplaces and stoves that had become a source of heat. They had warehoused vehicles in a yard and used the gas for chain saws until the fuel ran out.

During the last expedition, a young woman and her companion had been gone long enough to worry those who had remained behind. Upon their return, they revealed that to the east, there was a large Indigenous population that was continuing to follow the path of its ancestors. This news elated the People because such a group would be able to teach them how to survive.

As time passed, the generosity of the Anishinaabe people lent a kind of wisdom to daily life, and the People found a sort of equilibrium. These Amerindians kept greenhouses and were able to provide fresh vegetables and seeds for the new clan's gardeners. Each one helped the others according to his competencies; some nursed, fished, gathered edible or medicinal plants, built simple and easily heated homes, or fashioned instruments with whatever was at hand. Held in their memory were millions of years of human experience, from well before the species came to the end of its era. They thought about the actions to be taken, the initiatives likely to unite members of the community and guide them toward a certain feeling of serenity.

They gave the children lessons in mathematics, science, singing, martial arts, yoga, and meditation, the use of tools, carpentry – in short, any instruction that could prove useful.

Time had lost its parameters; with no calendar, they no longer identified the days or months. The sun's position gave them some sense of daily rhythm. The seasons, which had randomly overlapped since the Event, determined the years. What thoughts jostled about in each individual's mind? For some, developing into beings with no future was distressing. But not for Sam, a member of the Anishinaabe nation.

⤞⤝

The flakes fell from the clouds in light, fat flowers that floated in the air and landed on the hiker's hood. The snow formed a white dome that slid onto the ground when he bent down to tighten the snowshoe's rawhide strap around his moccasins. He stayed hunched over the ground for a long moment, admiring the delicate designs that his wife, Bella, had embroidered on the leather. For his, she chose masculine themes: a bear, a fir tree, or a sun, and usually adorned her needlework with stylized wild roses and leaves.

Bella had always been part of his universe. They were from the same community, the same band, and their families had adjoining hunting grounds, so that they moved together in the fall for the traditional trapping of fur-bearing animals. Sam had never doubted that they would one day be man and wife, even though their relationship seemed more like that of a brother with his little sister whom he loved to tease. A pretty girl with her plump cheeks and dark, laughing eyes, she had a slight lisp and called him "Zam" instead of "Sam." He smiled tenderly every time he heard this slight speech defect. Their marriage had been celebrated during the season of new flowers, and they were allotted a large portion of the two clans' territory, where they settled as soon as the season of falling leaves began. Their parents, worried about the consequences of the planetary imbalance, had advised against living so far from their families. But they had set out in their canoe, hauling a second craft loaded with items essential to the nomadic life.

As he raised the upper part of his body, Sam pushed back his beaver hat and offered his face up to the flakes, which he licked from his lips. The woods were muted by the slow, monochromatic barrage enveloping it in a mysterious aura. The black-trunked spruce trees lowered their branches to the ground, burdened by the weight of the pristine mass of relentlessly falling snow. Sometimes a hare crossed the trail, the movement of its lean body spotted by the man, who ignored it. When the time came to suspend his journey for the night, he would arm his bow with an arrow and kill an animal for his evening meal, unless he arrived at his destination today, which was highly unlikely. The loaded canoe attached by a wide strip of skin around his hips slowed his pace.

He had instinctively followed a path he had never taken, a shortcut along a river. He didn't know if its currents would be trapped under the ice or free to roil in great eddies, which would force him to backtrack. He hoped he'd be able to cross there. The seasons seemed to be returning to their normal pattern, and because that winter had been especially severe, the cold may have overpowered the impetuous waters.

He was distracted from his thoughts when he heard a baby's wailing coming from the canoe, followed by another feeble cry of hunger. Then his wife raised her voice. *"Ash ousta skoudè, Zam, abinoudishshish weemitzouth..."*

She asked her husband to stop and build a fire because she had to feed the babies.

Bella hadn't been feeling well since the birth of the twins, a girl and a boy. She had difficulty walking. For this reason, Sam was bringing her and the little ones back to their families. He had been keeping the three of them tucked under warm furs in the canoe. Worried about protecting them from the cold, he quickly raised a shelter over his wife and the infants.

The abundance of game animals was a blessing. Sam chewed on a bit of smoked meat that he kept in a bag slung across his body. He was tired because his family had spent the whole day on the move, except when answering the call of nature or caring for the babies. Bella melted snow in their aluminium pot, which her husband carried at his waist. Labrador tea leaves, kept dry in a tin box, were a luxury in this isolated place and a delight when the hot liquid ran all the way down the throat. The nomad took advantage of every moment when he felt energetic enough to pick up his pace, to scan his surroundings, to maintain his vigilance. He had slept little since leaving their encampment and feared a sudden thaw that would leave the lakes and rivers impassable.

As if the wind had guessed his thoughts, a sudden squall rushed through the trees. As it passed, it slapped the man's face, and he felt the air in his lungs grow colder. He raised his collar up to his nostrils. If the cold returned, the snow would form a crust on which the canoe would slide more easily, meaning less effort for his aching muscles.

After ensuring that his wife and children were comfortable, he set out again.

In autumn, before their departure, Bella's mother Emma had pulled Sam aside to try to persuade him to stay with the rest of the clan because she had guessed that her daughter was pregnant and wanted to keep the child.

"How will you manage if Bella has problems with her pregnancy?"

Emma did not understand her son-in-law, who insisted on living far from the family, an uncommon thing for his band's members to do and a decision that was not part of their traditions. The Anishinaabe lived as a group in the wintertime, for the health and safety of each individual.

The young couple had their reasons, believing that children would add meaning to their life, and not wanting to submit to pressure with regard to its choice to reproduce. Several women had decided to drink an abortifacient liquid concocted by a medicine woman named Annette Mackaw. This product acted much like the contraceptive pill of bygone days. Sam and Bella were surprised by the choice made by Anishinaabe *ikwes* since their people showed a deep respect for life and for children. But with people being mired in fear since the Event, attitudes had changed.

❧

For a week, Little Nibi had walked with more assurance. Kizik, her more skilled brother, walked through the village, smiling at everyone. The twins had become the joy of this cosmopolitan population, and everyone welcomed them with open arms. Their mother Bella had recovered, thanks to the care provided by their grandmother, Emma, and by Annette Mackaw. They guessed that the young woman and her husband would not be satisfied with just two children and that they would continue to enrich the People with new souls.

Meanwhile, couples had come together, including Abdullah and Kim, he of African origin and she of Chinese; and Roger, an Anishinaabe, and Erzulie, a Haitian. Among the women, the desire to reawaken their womb grew more tantalizing each day. For many of them, the biological clock was ticking down the hours because they had grown older during the past decade of uncertainty.

The People had become confident in its ability to survive; the upcoming generation showed mastery in all domains. The knowledge would be passed on.

><~><

There came a time when womanly curves proliferated among the People. Over the years, children of all possible shades of humankind enlivened households and the great multicultural village. They spoke several languages at once and mingled the words, thus inventing a unified language just as over time, they would create a human species free of the concept of race. They would benefit from the knowledge that their ancestors had bequeathed them. Stories told about the world before, as told by grandparents, would become legends to tell children at bedtime. The little ones enjoyed a certain tale in particular: the adventure of Sam and Bella, the couple who refused to relinquish the luminosity of children.

THE GREAT TREES

Michel Jean

Time passed, and little by little, her limbs grew stiff. It became unbearable. She could have chosen a more comfortable and accessible hideaway. Settling like her brother on the embankment, down where it was warm and where he was concealed by the lush grasses. That's what anyone else would have done. But she preferred to hide in the branches of a big tree. Her elevated position allowed her a bird's-eye view of the clearing, and it was easier to aim from above than from below. And arrows entered the flesh better when they were directed downward. Her grandfather had taught her that, as he had everything else she knew. But what was the point of having the best position if she couldn't hold it, if she couldn't stop moving, thereby revealing her presence? The blood was barely circulating through her benumbed muscles. She had been waiting since dawn, her back pressed against the trunk, a huntress among the leaves, and she enviously watched the grass where Kuuk waited for a game animal to appear. She sometimes wondered if it was not her pride that always drove her to do more than necessary.

The arms of the oak undulated in the wind that blew from the northeast. It was a giant whose highest point rose above all the others in the forest, and Juuk dared not guess how long it had been standing on the mountainside. Hundreds of years, according to her grandfather. This was surely true because the Elder knew everything. But imagining a life that stretched out over so many years made her dizzy; she was accustomed to measuring time according to the seasons.

"But as imposing as this one may be, it's a mere bush compared to the trees that touch the sky in the middle of the Southern Lake, if you consider how incredibly outsized they are. Nothing on the territory even comes close. Only the Creator knows the origin and the magic of the place."

The Great Trees. Juuk had heard talk of them since she was a child. According to legend, it took over a month to reach the lake over which they ruled. Their trunks sank into the water's depths, and they planted their roots in the heart of Mother Earth. She and Kuuk dreamed of travelling to the Great Trees together. But that was not likely to happen. Rare were the ones from the village who were able to go. Only the strongest and most courageous had the right to do so. "And the smartest, in particular," added her grandfather, for whom a person's value was measured more according to the strength of his mind rather than that of his arms.

It was the Elders who selected the chosen ones, and the honour had to be earned. Juuk would have liked to force their hand. See the Great Trees with her own eyes. Kuuk laughed when she spoke like that. Juuk's older brother, who was stronger than her, got on her nerves.

Juuk inhaled the earthy odours that rose from the ground. Filling her lungs. Forgetting the pain. Stop thinking about it. Waiting, silent as a stone. One leaf among thousands of others. The game would come. It had to come. She could still switch hiding places. There was a large branch a little lower down that would offer more comfortable shelter. But it wouldn't conceal her as well. Moreover, changing places would prove her brother right and show that she was one of those hunters who couldn't patiently absorb their pain.

By their very nature, nomads poorly tolerate immobility. Their bodies, particularly when they are young, felt the need to move, to track wild game. But her grandfather had taught her to blend in, disappear, to cease to exist, until the moment when she had to strike like lightning. Kuuk liked to hunt game from a canoe, to surprise an animal in the morning when it left the woods to drink. She had nothing but scorn for this way of doing things.

The hours passed, and the sun dipped behind the sea of vegetation that was its world, leaving rose-coloured clouds in its wake. How long had she been hanging onto this tree? Kuuk must have been asleep on the ground. Mastering his respiration. Becoming one with nature. Having the humility to recognize that it's the animal that offers itself up to enable man to live, and not the one who uses his skill to kill it. "We are no more important than the others. Each in its place, and man's place is beside the animals, not above them."

All around her, Juuk heard the noise of a squirrel's paws scratching the bark, the nervous flutter of birds' wings as they flitted from branch to branch. He who walks in the forest doesn't hear its song. Animals run away from him. One has to be quiet to hear life's heartbeat.

A cracking noise drew her out of her torpor. A simple cracking. One more sound in the forest's cacophony. A branch broken off by the wind, perhaps. The silence around her, interrupted by the aggressive chatter of a flock of blue jays. And still she listened, patient and unmoving. The huntress, her senses on alert, forgot the pain. Then she heard the delicate sound of a hoof stepping on the fertile soil. Almost nothing. Waiting, becoming one with the great tree. Finally, a proud and mighty stag emerged from the tall grass and came forward, swinging his antlers from right to left. He was confident but still wary. Other animals came out of the thicket – two females with the hair of their coat aquiver – and followed him. Then came another male, even bigger than the first, his coat whitened by the years. He stood a short distance away from the others. Juuk had never seen such an enormous caribou.

She pointed her bow in the lone animal's direction. She could shoot, but at this range, the wind could pull the arrow off course. She was waiting. Waiting and preparing herself. The old male moved slowly. She let him come closer. A few more steps. Juuk drew her bow, held her breath. Still waiting, blending in with the tree.

But before she could release her weapon's string, an arrow whistled through the tall grass. The caribou heard it and leapt forward. The projectile flew under the branches, barely missing its target, which ran toward the forest. Then everything happened quickly. The two females ran after the male and disappeared into the underbrush. The big male also ran, but away from the embankment, away from whence Kuuk's arrow had come.

Juuk kept her eyes on the big caribou, and at the very last second, she released her arrow. It traced an arc and struck the caribou just at the base his neck. Breathing heavily from his run, the animal seemed to hesitate for a moment, then his eyes clouded over and he collapsed, raising a cloud of dust. His blood stained the ground. Juuk began to breath again and thanked the caribou for his sacrifice, due to which the clan would eat.

She and her brother gutted and skinned the beast despite the fading light. It was hot, and they were more than two days away from the encampment. They decided to smoke the meat all night, right where they were. They hung the pieces over a fire fueled by dead wood. Meanwhile, they retrieved the skin, and carefully cleaned and dried it. Juuk thought of the clothing her mother would make with the caribou leather.

In the morning, the brother and sister began to walk, hanging the animal's bones on branches to leave behind them as an homage. The trail ran along a winding river and wove around mountains whose peaks were lost in the clouds. They moved forward with assurance, accustomed as they were since childhood to steep paths. They slept under the stars, in a hurry to get to their destination. At the end of the third day, the tent village finally appeared on the banks of a lake with rough waters.

The family welcomed them; their mother embraced them. The clan's elder smiled when he saw the heavy sacks that his grandchildren had brought back. That evening, they all enjoyed a meal of boiled rabbit and dried caribou meat. Their mother had saved them a bit of blueberries in bear grease. The fire crackled in the night, and they ate under the light of the full moon. A successful hunt was an occasion to celebrate.

After the meal, the grandfather – who up until then had listened attentively to Kuuk's account of the expedition – began to speak. The others grew silent.

"As you know, every 10 years, a clan is chosen to make the trip to the Great Trees. A member of that clan is permitted to go on behalf of his family and his community. The Council has determined that it is our turn this year. I went a long time ago. Your father, Kuuk and Juuk, also went; may his soul be with the Creator. It is an honour that the family humbly accepts. It is easy to get to the Great Trees. But it takes a great deal of courage and wisdom to return. Several have lost their lives there."

Juuk, excited by the idea that her clan had been chosen, listened to the old man's gravelly voice. The Elder had never revealed what he had seen during his voyage. Nor had her father. She hadn't known him well since he had been killed by a starving bear that had attacked their camp when she was just 10 years old. All sorts of stories were told about that forbidden place. But the few who had seen it with their own eyes did not speak of it.

"As for me, I almost didn't make it back. But I was young and determined. You must venture across an expanse of water the likes of which you've never even imagined. A lake that reaches all the way to the horizon. The most important thing is knowing when to brave it. If the wind kicks up, the unwary will be lost. The lake will swallow man and canoe. And no one will hear of him again. This is what happened to Ak, of the Nan clan, last summer."

Juuk had know Ak well. He had been a young and gifted hunter with boundless energy. He had a gentle, confident look in his eyes. His disappearance had saddened many.

And Ak's mother had not recovered from it. Apparently, she could often be heard at night, cursing the Great Trees for taking her son.

"To be honest, I would have preferred not to have to choose," continued the old man, his voice a monotone. "I would prefer not to send anyone from my family."

"But I want to go…" hissed Kuuk, clenching his fists.

Juuk's brother was the biggest and strongest of the village's young men. She considered his ambition to be justified.

"This is not a game, my son, nor is it a gift," interrupted the Elder, silencing him with a simple wave of the hand. "It is more of a curse. And know this: the only prize to be brought back is wisdom."

Juuk watched her grandfather. With his eyes closed, the old man appeared to be concentrating, or perhaps praying to the Creator. "This man has everyone's respect. Having been sent on this adventure during his own youth, he knows better than anyone the sacrifice that he's about to ask of my brother," thought Juuk. What wisdom was he speaking of? She didn't know, but she was convinced that if any hunter was ready to meet the challenge, it was her brother.

The old man raised his arms toward the star-studded sky, as if imploring the Almighty.

"My choice is based on all the wisdom that remains to me. You are the one who will go to the Great Trees," he continued, indicating Juuk with his right hand. "May the Creator guide and protect you, my daughter."

The water pulsated at the river's surface. Juuk paddled rhythmically. Each stroke of the oar took her further from home and nearer her destiny. In the past six weeks, there had been only three days without rain, and her constantly wet clothing irritated her skin and hindered her movements. The little stream flowing between the mountains, on which she'd started out at the beginning of summer, had gradually become a majestic river that now flowed slowly through a thick forest.

Despite the bad weather, she had kept up her pace, refusing to wait for the sun. And one evening, as the light faded, the terrifying lake suddenly appeared around one final bend.

She pitched her tent a fair distance from the shore where it would be sheltered from the wind. There among the trees, she felt as if she were surrounded by her own people. Juuk swallowed a bit of dried meat, while outside the lake rumbled, and powerful waves rose from the depths and threw themselves angrily onto the sand. The wind shook the treetops, the rain clawed the skins of her shelter. She waited in silence. Forgot fear. Stayed humble in the face of the elements. Became invisible. Melted into the forest until just the right time.

For five days and five nights, the cold hard rain fell. The wind tore at the lake, and the white-crested waves rode its dark surface. Juuk sometimes stood on the beach, letting the gusts blowing off the huge lake bite her skin. Filling her with their strength. Becoming nothing but a part of nature. She waited.

On the sixth day, she woke at dawn to a strange silence. In the east, the sun cast jets of bright light on the water. Its rage spent, the lake had dropped off to sleep. Juuk could have waited a few days to be certain that the clement weather would hold, but the mild air, the unmoving forest, and especially the sun's presence reassured her. She had to take advantage of the sleep of that which she feared the most.

Juuk tossed her day's provisions into her canoe, filled her skin with water, and set out straight ahead, directly south, thereby following her grandfather's instructions. He had told her that in clear weather, you could see the Great Trees from the shore, but the morning mist still clung to the milky horizon. She knew that the journey would be long and perilous.

"It will take you at least five hours to get there. Pay attention. Watch the sky. At the slightest change, turn around and go back. The lake does not forgive those who defy it. It will allow you passage only while it sleeps. Then go quickly and quietly, Juuk."

Throughout her youth, she had learned at his side through observation. By listening and watching. The Elders taught by example, and one had to remain humble before their knowledge. But that evening, her grandfather took her aside and spoke to her as he never had before, giving a detailed explanation of the dangers that awaited her, the traps that she would have to avoid. Then he went to talk with Kuuk, who had been stunned to hear his sister's name. After all, wasn't he the strongest in the entire village? What advantage did she offer to have merited this honour? And what had he done to have proven unworthy? The Elder had given no justification for his choice. He had simply said that Juuk was resilient, clever, and most of all, that she had a talent for feeling things, a talent that she would badly need. The young man had accepted the decision, even though it cost him dearly. His affection for his sister had helped him overcome his jealousy.

She paddled agilely and in silence. The boat traced a straight line across the dark stretch. The forest she'd left behind was no more than a thin strip of green that faded away as Juuk travelled further into the infinite and disappeared into the unknown. Here, her sturdy canoe, which she had built with her own hands, was nothing more than a fragile strip of bark at the mercy of wind or storm. She travelled without stopping, swallowing a little dried meat at regular intervals and drinking water to keep up her strength. She remained focussed. She was breathing calmly. Pacing herself. Trying not to wake the beast. Waiting. Waiting for the Great Trees to appear before her. The midday sun warmed the lake's surface and gradually swept away the mist, revealing a landscape of incomparable beauty.

Dozens of giants of different shapes and sizes emerged from the water and appeared to touch the sky. The sun was reflected off of their seemingly unreal trunks.

Juuk, as fascinated as she was frightened, rowed toward the forest. How could these astonishing creatures stand right in the middle of the water? It was beyond all comprehension. All lined up, the titans formed aqueous paths along which her canoe, like a dwarf in the land of giants, advanced carefully. Above her head, flocks of big white birds flew over the vertiginous spires. Some of them, having managed to perch on some kind of ledge, regarded her with disdain. Their cries got lost in the vast expanses. Everything here seemed to be of immense proportions: the endless lake, the formidable trees, the animals that resembled no others.

It had taken her five hours to reach the marine forest. And now? What was the meaning of this mysterious place? What must she understand? She hesitated over the sequence of events. Should she wait? Make herself invisible? But how was she to melt into this forest where the only trace of life was the birds watching her from a distance? In their woods, at their camp, the scents of earth and grass blended with those emitted by the trunks of trees. Here, she smelled nothing but salty water, making her feel like a stranger. Was it only about the trees? Or was it instead about malevolent creatures petrified in the middle of the lake?

Her canoe came to a halt before one of the giants. The sun cast glowing lines of green and blue upon it. Minutes passed. She knew that her time was limited, but still she waited. For what, she did not know. The place was an enigma that had been imposed on her and that she was required to solve.

Suddenly, something moved nearby. With one quick gesture, she put her palm on the knife she wore at her hip. She held her breath. Apart from those filthy animals squawking above her head, who or what might inhabit this mournful site? Who was playing tricks on her? Who was hiding in the shadows? She would have liked to call out. Shout her fear. But her grandfather's words came back to her. Lie low. Blend into the environment. Become one with it. She was no longer alone. He was at her side, reassuring her. Her breathing slowed. Her pulse returned to its normal rhythm. She must not awaken the lake. She caressed the water with her paddle. She remained invisible and moved forward quietly, ignoring the white birds' piercing refrain.

She sought. She scrutinized. She thought she saw the shadow at the bend, picked up her weapon, and drew near. But she realized that what she had taken for an intruder was only her own reflection. The surface of one of the trees mirrored back her own image, as would a freshwater river. How was that possible? The canoe glided up to the foot of the Great Tree. She laid a hand on its perfectly smooth surface. Her fingers left a mark, which she immediately wiped away. When she rubbed, a strange phenomenon occurred: the tree revealed its interior. Juuk was troubled; she had never seen such magic. But curiosity got the best of her, and again she rubbed her hand across the hard surface, which became translucent, exposing its heart.

Juuk cupped a hand around either side of her face and then stuck her hands against the outer wall to get a better look at the giant's belly. Strangely, what she saw resembled a ceiling and a residence's floor on which whitish objects seemed to have been thrown in disarray. Using a little water, she rubbed again and put her face back between her hands.

Her stomach tightened, and she felt nauseated. What she had thought were pieces of wood bleached by the years and scattered on the floor were actually human bones. She blinked her eyes, inhaled the air. "Wait. Stay calm. Do not wake the beast," she told herself

Before her eyes were dozens of human skeletons. Some formed circles; others, over to one side, had fallen in front of the outer wall, as if these men and women had chosen to die alone. There were tens, hundreds, so numerous that she couldn't count them all.

Juuk's heart raced. She resisted the urge to flee and moved toward the next tree, a grey one, circular in shape. She cleaned the outer wall. It too was filled with human remains. Juuk passed from one giant to the next, and each time the scene repeated itself. Who were these people? Where had they come from? Why had they lived here? Were the Great Trees nothing but tombs?

And what if that which she had assumed were trees were nothing but a forgotten world's monstrous dwellings that had been submerged by the great flood the Elders spoke of, and where now tens of thousands of humans were slowly turning back to dust? The cry of the birds drew her out of her stupor. The birds, the only living things in that place.

She had to leave, and quickly. Juuk pointed her canoe northward. She began to paddle with all her might and convinced herself not to scream out of revulsion and fear. "Stay calm, do not awaken the lake, leave the giants in their silence." Sweat stung her eyes, soaked her clothes, but she maintained her rhythm and stayed on course. At some point, a quivering swept across the water. The wind picked up. The giant had awakened. It knew she was there.

Juuk paddled harder. Her muscles pulled; she struggled to breathe. She paddled to save her life. Fear was catching up to her. A fear that she had never known. The lake began to ripple and roll, and it would soon set the canoe to dancing. She didn't have enough time. The riverbank before her seemed so far away! She paddled with every ounce of energy she had. She would have liked to have Kuuk's strength, so she could move faster.

The wind bit at the water's surface. Waves slapped the bark like a drum beating a sinister song carried by the wind. The canoe dipped, hesitated, rose up again. Water entered the canoe and made manoeuvring it increasingly difficult. Juuk tried to bail with one hand and paddle with the other. If she stopped moving, she'd be lost. Only the canoe's forward movement enabled her to avoid the fury of the elements. The horizon grew hazy. How long had she been rowing? She had lost all notion of time. Alone on this cursed lake, she would end up like all those men and women back there, swallowed by the depths, a prisoner of the trees for all eternity.

The wind hit her and threw torrents of water in her face, choking her. She was going to sink. Then as one final wave lifted her high into the air, a hand rose up and kept the canoe from capsizing. Another steady hand gripped the gunwale and pulled her toward shore. She heard a strong, reassuring voice. "You'll be fine, Juuk, you'll be fine."

Kuuk guided her back to solid ground, pressed her benumbed body against him. Her brother had followed her and waited on the beach. Without him, she would still be wandering the icy depths. Kuuk put a pelt around his sister's shoulders. He carried her into the tent where a fire was burning. The warmth eased Juuk's fears, chased away the darkness that gripped her heart. Kuuk asked no questions. He was there. Exhausted, she fell asleep near the flames. She dreamt of giants and skeletal prisoners. Of the birds that had tried to prevent her escape.

In the morning, Kuuk prepared the meal. He served her hot tea.

"You scared me. How did you manage to get through that storm in a canoe? How could anyone have kept that boat balanced on the waves. I couldn't believe it when I saw you coming. You scared me to death, little sister."

Juuk pulled the fur a little tighter around her, swallowed some of the drink, which spread a bit of warmth through her. She thought about her forest, her world.

"Let's go," she said. "It's time to go home."

SKIN COLOURS

JEAN SIOUI

An expedition of White men dropped anchor in Kanata in 1534, believing they'd reached India. A large assembly awaited them upon their arrival. Some, in bark canoes, paddled around the sailing ship while others watched from the shore. All the men had red faces. According to their traditions, the Iroquois smeared their faces with ochre on certain occasions. At Stadacona, the Europeans saw what they thought were Indians beneath this ceremonial paint.

The men from the ship were clothed in curious garb. They were filthy and reeked like the bottom of the ship's hold, an odour unfamiliar to the country's inhabitants. They also spoke a strange language. They said words that smelled of fear and made nervous gestures in greeting. Their skin was pale; they appeared to be ill.

They came off the sailing ship and never left. Save for the captain, who headed back out to sea. His body was found frozen found in a glacier. They stayed on the land that they claimed to have discovered.

>~~-<

On January 1, 2234, an abnormal phenomenon surprised the White population. The insidious reawakening of an unknown virus that spread rapidly throughout the entire country. Scientists baptized the virus Vanora-blue or Pox-7. They believed it to be a new mutation of smallpox, which had decimated the Wendat nation early in the 17th century. The epidemic affected all children who were descendants of the first colonists, who had brought smallpox in their great sailing ships. A disease that, at the time, had severely afflicted the Huron-Wendat people. An abomination that had travelled around Mother Earth for several years. Now, Pox-7 attacked Kanata's newborns. White babies were born blue, while Red babies remained white.

It was enough to revive the horrors of a time best forgotten. Once again in 2234, the RCMP took Wendat families by force. Upon orders from the federal government, it stole children away from their family and forced them into their medical laboratories. Scientists did their utmost, trying to learn why all the babies in the country except for the Wendat were born with blue skin.

⤙⤚

In the beginning of the 2000s, governments had been discussing forgiveness and reconciliation with Indigenous peoples. At the start of 2270, 36 years after the onset of the epidemic, the Indigenous were still the victims of prejudice and systemic racism. Nearly 40 years of living with the new virus, politicians, conspiracy theorists, and the media shamelessly accused the Wendat nation of witchcraft. They claimed that shamans had cast a spell on Canadians, seeking revenge for their inaction after several studies, numerous government reports, and a variety of promises had gone unheeded. Promises that should still have corrected the injustices committed against the First Nations. Since the beginning of the epidemic, many of the Elders had died, and the young people had taken up the talking stick. Before the new generation of blue-skinned Whites, they vociferously predicted the consequences of the great injuries inflicted upon the earth.

In squalid laboratories, newborns, adolescents, adults, and the elderly – Wendats of every generation – were held prisoner. White-skinned young scientists and a few rare old doctors studied the Wendats' physiology. The researchers committed atrocities against the bodies of the Indigenous. Horrific experiments were carried out in these laboratories: biopsies, surgeries, injections of experimental medications, and even the desecration of human remains.

One day, a Wendat doctor and father of seven children was bathing his baby and wondered about the brown spot in the middle of his son's back. He remembered that the Elders had called this spot "the Indian birthmark." His seven children each had one.

Why did the Wendat have this mark? What was its origin? The medicine man from Wendake's Bear Clan wanted to find the answers to his questions. In his culture, the bear symbolized the Wendat people's traditional medicine. It was thus in the spirit of the bear that he would find a solution to the evil that was afflicting the country. He had to walk in the bears' tracks. The medicine man decided to take his family to live in isolation on his ancestors' land. He, his wife, and his children went to Lac des Neiges where they spent a period of time, meditating at the family's old trapping camp.

There, in a cupboard, he discovered a dusty book, excerpts from which his father had read to him when he was very young. A book on the wisdom of the Elders. His father had told him that it had been written by a great Wendat prophet.

The book predicted that the flesh of the men who destroy nature will suffer an affliction. It said that only the guardians of Mother Earth would escape this fate. One of the nation's shamans had altered their DNA, implanting a gene taken from an animal species that had disappeared as a result of global warming. This was to protect them from the gods' punishment. The birthmark on the children's back was to be the hallmark of this genetic alteration.

The book also foretold that one day in the distant future, they would have to invite the blue-skinned men onto their ancestral lands so that these men could atone for having harmed the earth and receive the great Spirit's forgiveness.

When the medicine man returned to the city and revealed the prophecy to the population, hundreds of young Canadians went up to Lac des Neiges, in the heart of Wendat territory. Several acknowledged that they had shown disrespect for nature. All those who repented were healed; their skin again became white, like the rabbit's fur when winter is nigh. Those who stubbornly refused to admit that nature had suffered from their disregard and insisted that economic development at any cost was modern society's priority remained blue-skinned and, in fact, the colour grew even deeper.

As a result of the medicine man's discovery, the labs were closed, and the children returned to their community, telling of the injuries they had sustained. Once again, the government proffered false justifications. Racism persisted; it was on the rise. First Nations were accused of having tried to destroy the world – a world being subjected to reckless development.

Now, the majority of babies born to all the nations of Kanata have innocent, and therefore white, skin. There is a certain resurgence of respect for nature. One day soon, there might be a return to the unconditional protection of Mother Earth, as demanded by the voice of First Nations. A lack of discipline will no longer have its place among us. World leaders will even discuss this at the summit. Nevertheless, the earth still protests its many wounds.

What will tomorrow bring? By what colour skin shall we know each other? Will we be *yaronhhia' ïohti, öndienhta' ïohti*, or *wenta' ïohti*? Blue, white, or red?

PAKAN (DIFFERENTLY)

Cyndy Wylde

Her head is buzzing, it's humid, it's dark, she cannot move, but she feels calm. Maïka wonders where she is. Her memory is spotty. A few moments ago, she felt as if she were in free fall. Suddenly she experiences intense abdominal pain, as if her guts were tearing apart inside her. She begins to cough to eject whatever is blocking her throat. She chokes it up and expels liquid, and this is painful. Maïka is well aware that she is spitting up water.

Kepek, 2022

Quebec as Kanena knew it no longer existed. The population struggled to recover from a global pandemic that had lasted far too long. The economic consequences were indescribable, most businesses had gone bankrupt, the unemployment rate was at an historic level, and a great many people were psychologically fragile, if not on the edge of the abyss.

The Prime Minister acted like the paterfamilias at first, but over time, he took his measures too far and treated the population like children. Under his stewardship, the government subjected its citizens to a regimented way of life. Domination gradually took hold, with complete acquiescence and no questions asked. Wishing to "do their part," all citizens docilely obeyed the New Regulations that were imposed, for sanitary reasons at the outset. But two years later, it had to be admitted that democracy was dead and that absolute power ruled the day. Citizens were too beaten down to fight back.

Kanena was no exception. This period had been difficult for her. She was a member of the Anishinaabe nation and, although she had lived in an urban setting for a long time, she had witnessed a new decline in her people's living conditions due to the pandemic. This pandemic, like those that had come before, shone a spotlight on social inequities. From the beginning, First Nation peoples had endured many hardships, and many of them were barely surviving. This reality was true for Indigenous people across the country.

Who would have believed that what was going to happen would go beyond everything her people had had to survive up until then?

Although still in her early 30s, Kanena had already witnessed both the evolution and the stagnation of living conditions and, from across the country, she heard her people's grievances. She was among those who'd had the courage to participate in various resistance movements and had seen some of their positive, if transitory, results. Whether it was to denounce the traumatizing and intergenerational effects of Indian residential schools and to address the situation, to help counter one of the government's outrageous legal remedies for dealing with the system for protecting First Nations children, to confirm and condemn recourse to the forced sterilization of Indigenous women, to demand that multinationals stop inserting their gas and oil pipelines into Mother Earth, or always, always to educate the people, Kanena had been a tireless activist her entire life.

Although she had seen certain solidarity movements among Quebeckers who wanted to change things, discrimination and racism were always present. After the pandemic, she noted that public services had always been tainted by these issues, as had been educational institutions. To her great dismay, Kanena found that government authorities were not ready for the shift that she and her people had hoped for all their lives. This pandemic had quintupled the size of the gap that separated the Indigenous from Quebeckers. Kanena had so hoped that mutual support would prevail, but that is not what happened.

Kepek, 2042

Nibi returned from the hospital, shaken by the news she'd just received. She was carrying a child. How was this possible? She had never had sexual relations. People had given up their religious belief in immaculate conceptions and virgin births ages ago. Trying to put her thoughts in order, she figured she had only one option: to consult another doctor. But who? Where?

Since the last pandemic, which had occurred before she was born, hospitals had been built for the Indigenous. Her mother told her that at the time, members of First Nations had advocated for the creation of these institutions so that their people could be treated with dignity when it came to health care. Indigenous peoples hoped to see an end to the racism that they too often experienced. These hospitals were to be places where language no longer constituted a barrier and where the cultural aspects of different First Nations were taken into consideration. Moreover, these institutions were to finally fall in line with the sincere goal of affirmation and self-determination by putting in place an entirely Indigenous governing body. Nibi remembered hearing Kanena hold forth on the subject with energy and conviction... her mother was a true warrior. She had learned to defend her people with words, with laws, and with education.

Although the intentions behind the creation of these hospitals were highly commendable, the reality was somewhat different from the dream. The pandemic had caused an economic upheaval from which it was difficult to recover, and the first victims were those who already lived in precarious conditions. Indigenous people were ranked at the top of the list. This led to staggering drop-out rates and unemployment numbers, and several other situations meant that jobs intended to be filled by First Nations people in these medical establishments were never held by them.

The Centre-South Hospital was named Manadjiwewin, which means "respect" in Anishinaabe. This was where Nibi had to go, as determined by her band number. Since its founding, it had been staffed solely by non-Indigenous doctors. The same was true for almost all the other positions. Nibi was born in this hospital. She knew it well. She'd received health care there throughout her life, from the first vaccination to the first dental appointment, and including all her routine annual visits. So, where should she go? Who should she ask? Her mother would have been able to guide her and help her understand what was happening to her.

But Kanena had disappeared one day, leaving not a trace. Nibi had certainly tried to explain to the authorities that her mother would never have abandoned her with no warning, but no one in the police department was concerned by her disappearance. Nibi was appalled by this reaction. People were totally indifferent when it came to the disappearance of an Indigenous woman.

Nibi sighed in exasperation when she thought back on it. Keeping silent in the face of her anger and powerlessness was becoming a habit.

Kepek, 2043

Nibi studied the envelope in the mailbox. Humidity had made the crinkled paper a bit damp. She inhaled deeply and decided that she really should open it. It was the third letter from the minister in charge of Indigenous issues. Already knowing what it would say, she grabbed the envelope with the firm intention to have done with it. Because it was a lost cause; she was sure of it. Her eyes immediately fell on the last paragraph:

[...] subject to section 6, a person is entitled to be registered. However, in compliance with the provisions of the Indian Act, we must reject the application to register your child. It is understood that if one of the parents of a person is registered by virtue of subsection 6(2) and the other parent is unknown or unregistered, said person is ineligible for registration.

Nibi crumpled the paper and looked at Maïka. "Well now," she thought. "Your fate is sealed, my love. Our line-

age, as far as the government is concerned, ends with you."
It infuriated her to think that the bureaucrat who wrote that
letter shamelessly contradicted himself. She knew that it
would be impossible to prove anything because so many
records had been interpreted to suit the Crown. Father
unknown; no Indigenous status can be expected. Period,
end of sentence.

She held her daughter tenderly in her arms and kissed
the little red mark near her ear: "It doesn't matter. Believe
me, you're Anishinaabe, now and forever."

Kepek, June 21, 2063, 10:30 a.m.

Feeling queasy, Maïka went to the sink where she had
left the stick from the pregnancy test. When she saw the
result, she immediately had the urge to vomit. She leaned
over to the right and emptied everything that it was possible to empty from her slim body. She was pregnant. A baby
was growing in her belly. She grabbed her cell phone and
said, "Mom." The phone rang once, twice.

"*Kuei*, dear, how are you?"

Maïka answered bluntly, "You're going to be a *kokom*,
Mom."

Nibi had expected instead to hear, "Mom, I got into law
school, so are we celebrating?" They had both been waiting
for the answer to her applications. Put on the spot, all she
could think of to say to her daughter was, "Okay… and how
did that happen?"

"It's impossible, Mom! Not only do I still have an IUD,
but I haven't been with anyone since Jay. Remember? He's
been out of my life for a year now."

"Wait for me, I'll be right there!"

Barely 20 minutes later, a bewildered-looking Nibi arrived at Maïka's.

"History is repeating itself. This is no coincidence, that much is obvious."

Nibi calmly recounted how she had known that she was pregnant with Maïka and told her what her research had uncovered. None of the children of Maïka's generation had been able to get Indian status. The network of women activists that she worked with had tried to find answers, and several scientists had arrived at some disturbing conclusions. Nibi explained to her daughter how much she would have liked to avoid having this conversation. Despite all the details she knew at that point, her daughter was the apple of her eye and the flesh of her flesh. Having status or not, according to the government's standards, meant nothing in Anishinaabe. But Nibi was certain that Maïka had to know the truth, so that she in turn could choose her own future.

"I have something to tell you, but not here. Let's go walk along the river."

Nibi was aware that government monitoring had been increased following the pandemic of 2020. Everything was recorded, either by household appliances now manufactured accordingly or by the rays emanating from the municipal lighting system. There was even an anonymous tip line for citizens wishing to denounce a neighbour or colleague they suspected of failing to comply with the various policies set since 2020. For a reason that would become increasingly clear – namely the need to control them – Indigenous people were under particularly close surveillance. The hospitals built for them were inevitably bugged, as were other establishments, most notably the prisons.

It was therefore likely that everything would be heard, but the current regime's officials came up against one barrier: Indigenous languages. Nibi made it her business to teach her language to Maïka. All the Indigenous people of her generation who were parents had done the same. The revitalization of their identity was a driving force, but it operated in the shadows to avoid arousing the wrath of the State. Nibi herself had had to employ several ruses to preserve her mother tongue. Born to parents who had been sent to residential schools where their Indigenous identity was targeted for destruction by prohibiting the use of their language, Nibi had promised herself that she would honour her ancestors and perpetuate her own. She had managed to keep Anishinaabe alive and well with her daughter and, on that day, the privacy that it allowed would help her preserve something equally vital.

Kepek, June 21, 2063, 12:30 p.m.

The two women walked at the water's edge, aware that there was little risk of being listened to, or at least of being understood. By speaking Anishinaabe, Nibi added an obstacle to comprehension that reassured her. Suddenly, she stopped and looked Maïka right in the eye.

"Your unknown father is truly unknown."

When her daughter gave her a puzzled look, she continued. "He is unknown because he does not exist."

Nibi went on gently, "When I was born, they inserted a chip here, behind this red dot, near my ear. I'll explain later how I made this discovery, but the reasons why this chip was inserted without my knowledge, and also without my mother's knowledge, are both simple and complicated."

Maïka recognized the same little red scar that she had as well. She had never noticed that they had this in common and guessed that her mother had deliberately hidden it from her. Nibi sighed deeply and explained that her generation had understood that the genocide of Indigenous peoples was being carried out on a daily basis. She shared with Maïka what she had discovered up until then.

"As Quebec's population was trying its best to recover from the worldwide pandemic, times were tough for Indigenous peoples throughout the province and across the whole country. For many, they represented a significant economic burden on society in addition to being an increasingly serious impediment when it came to developing territories and accessing natural resources.

She reminded her daughter how Canada and the provinces had, for over 150 years, employed every means possible to make the Indigenous disappear. Despite every use of deception and all the stratagems tried by the State, the Indigenous had not only resisted but they had grown stronger and stronger, thus becoming a formidable challenge to government. The members of First Nations were more numerous due to a higher birth rate in comparison to the rest of the population. Many were also getting a better education now that they had flooded into the institutions of learning.

Then the pandemic had challenged the authority of the government system in place, and renewing the people's ideological adhesion became essential, particularly on the economic level, which was and always would be the key to winning the electorate's heart.

"The Quebec government proved to be a national leader. By repeatedly ignoring all the debates and issues related to the province's Indigenous people, and even ignoring lawful demands issued by the court in various cases, it had insidiously instituted a practice in the hospitals meant to serve us. Under threat of being fired, doctors were ordered to insert a programmed chip in every Indigenous baby beginning in 2022, the year I was born. This procedure was done with the greatest secrecy. It wasn't hard to do considering the State's complete control of information. The chips ensure a programmed pregnancy within 18 to 25 years of their insertion. Another chip is inserted into children born as a result of this process. With an unknown father, these children no longer have the right to be included in the Indian Register. They are quite simply unrecognized in the eyes of the law. The government frees itself of any obligation to them, especially an economic one."

Nibi explained to her daughter that she was convinced this ploy would remain in place until there was not a single First Nations person nor a single Inuit left in the country. The State's access to land and economic relief depended on it.

Weary, she muttered, "This is history repeating itself."

Kepek, June 21, 2063, 2:30 p.m.

Maïka struggled to breathe. Her head was spinning. She was perspiring, her mouth was dry, and she felt the anger rising inside. She knew well this anger that made her heart pound. She verged on anger on a daily basis, like any number of her people. Anger that made her want to shout at the entire world, "Just who do you take us for? On whose behalf do you act so heartlessly? You have flooded my ancestors' territory with your hydroelectric dams for money, you have destroyed our forests for money, you have killed off the moose, the caribou, and the salmon for money; and for money, you have invaded Mother Earth with your gas and oil pipelines…"

Maïka didn't realize it, but she was shouting out loud, a cry that came from deep in her belly. She began to run. She had no idea where she was heading, but she had to escape this terribly ugly world, a world where the government was again committing horrible acts for the sake of money. She ran and ran. She remembered images of her once nomadic people, she remembered her mother's smile as she whispered words in her beloved language, but she smelled the odour of burning oil from the refineries. She fell into the water…

Mikinak (turtle)

Maïka feels transported… she feels as if she's been floating for an eternity. When she opens her eyes, she sees wings folding out from the sides of her body. She is flying, but it is thanks to the magnificent Canada geese carry her. They place her on the back of a turtle swimming in the middle of what appears to be the ocean. Suddenly, Maïka recognizes the muskrat from her childhood and knows the story: the legend about how the world was created. In the depths are former villages that were flooded by the government. Her ancestors had lived and given birth there. Maïka can feel the force of their presence, their souls that accompany her. She inhales deeply and smiles.

She knows that soon the muskrat will be joined by other animals that live in the water who, like him, will be holding moist soil in their paws. The turtle will allow a larger and larger area covered with these bits of earth to be attached to him. Turtle Island will be reborn, and Maïka will become the grandmother of all the human beings on this new earth.

Mikinak (turtle) and *Wazhashk* (muskrat)

The rivers are beautiful and clean. You can safely drink the water. The salmon jump, the rutting and reproductive periods of the moose are again protected, the polar bear regains its strength. The Forest Alert comes to an end, the ice stops melting, everyone's allergies disappear, real life resumes its natural course. On a night with a full moon, Mikinak and Wazhashk ask the Creator why he has made this new work, the second turtle, the second Mother Earth.

The Creator responds in a calm and sober tone. "I indulged the human. The destruction would never end, and the first turtle's back could no longer tolerate the pain that was being inflicted upon it. Despite the fact that the Earth was showing signs of increasing distress, nothing was done to keep it from suffering. So I saved the villages flooded here and replanted forests that had been clear-cut; I fostered conditions necessary for the survival of the caribou, moose, polar bears, salmon, and several plants here. For years, I have been preserving everything that the White man destroyed, looking forward to better days. After 170 years, I realized that it would be impossible to save the first Mother Earth and that it would be better to recreate *pakan* – differently – this time. The first Mother Earth, such as you knew it, was falling apart.

"You are the protectors of the turtle. You belong to it; it does not belong to you. From now on, evil must not be allowed to take so much space on its back. Protect Mother Earth. This entire responsibility, I entrust to you."

2091

Elisapie Issac

Tayara came from the North, from a spit of land squeezed between two massive bays. One was known by its traditional name, Ungava. The other had been renamed some 50 years earlier. It was no longer known by the name of the White man who claimed to have discovered it, but by the name given by the people who lived there: Tutjaani Bay.

He was handsome, not the kind of handsome that you see, but rather the kind that you feel. He had an imposing presence. He had all the characteristics of an Inuk man. He was affable, and the look in his eyes was shot through with a tender sadness, while still being proud and straight as an arrow, and it never failed to touch hearts. It made you feel like you were in familiar territory; there was no judgement in his gaze.

Tayara worked for Imak Tourism, a tour operator that had developed a White clientele. This government-owned company had been created in the 2030s and had contributed to the region's economic growth. Over the years, its large profits had been injected into Nunavik's scientific research chair.

He was at ease, in his element; he welcomed the tourists arriving from the South and took them on a boat tour of Nunavik. He had been a cultural guide for almost eight years. He had his own routine when tourists came aboard.

"*Ai, tungasugitsi Nunavimmi,* welcome to Nunavik. Nunavik means 'the place where we live.' I will be your guide, I'm here for you, I am very familiar with this territory, its fauna. I'll be here to answer your questions during this two-week trip, which we'll be taking according to the rhythm of the waters flowing from the North and according to our community's traditional stories. I'll tell you right up front, we're in no hurry.

"My name is Tayara, forget about my last name, it's not important, it was the *qallunaaq*, the White people, who assigned us last names back in the 20th century when they decided that assigning numbers was sort of inhumane!" he laughed.

"My first name can be traced back over seven generations, and probably even further than that. My grandfather's great-grandfather was also called Tayara. Our names are very important here. They form the line that comes from the past, and they help us connect all the previous generations to us and to our descendants. When we carry on the name of our ancestors, we carry on their characteristics, as if their souls return and live on in us. It's a kind of reincarnation. Those who share the same name, we call each other *saunik*, which means 'bone.' As if we share this thing that remains when we've eaten every bit of an animal's flesh.

"I have plenty of *saunik* around here because there are several Tayaras. And if you conceive a baby on this voyage, I hope he'll be my *saunik*!"

Charmed by the young man, the tourists laughed out loud. They all felt reassured and already unconsciously felt a blind confidence in their guide.

Aputik, that last to be hired on the team of guides, listened attentively to Tayara. She thought she could easily match his sense of humour. She wondered how old he was. He didn't seem to be much older than she, no more than 30. She was intrigued by his excessive confidence, which she considered to be a bit "over the top." She had just turned 26. The other guides were older; some were even in their 60s. They were almost elders and had a great deal of experience. They were calmer; they were hunters who would surely teach her all sorts of things.

Tayara continued his presentation. Aputik found it to be a bit long. He was clearly a good storyteller because the tourists were captivated. Many of the women were smiling from ear to ear. He was not mistaken – the women were impressed; they had come to their favourite holiday camp. The North had a way of awakening the senses and the emotions.

"My *saunik* Tayara from seven generations ago also welcomed people from the South, except that his visitors were the first *qallunaaq*, the first White people to come. He guided for geologists, anthropologists, and archeologists. He used a dog sled or a boat to ferry them around. My family comes from Salluit, which is located on the isthmus between the two bays. The place is incredible, one of the most beautiful fjords in the country. You will definitely see the humungous crater along the Kangiqsujuaq road. But this year, the highlight will be the festival of Sinaani, which means 'beach.' This year is very special because we're celebrating the 50th anniversary of the rene-gotiation of the James Bay Agreement, which declared the independence of Nunavik as an autonomous province. I assume you're already aware of the programming many of your favourite Inuit and Indigenous artists will be there.

"Another highlight for science fans who want to learn about the local fauna is the research centre managed by my big sister, Alacie. She directs the research chair that helps us maintain the region's permafrost. I'm sure she will be able to answer all your questions. Every year she tells me she's going to work on her grumpy face, but I can't promise you anything." He imagined his sister would kill him for saying that. "But don't take it personally, it's just that she's very shy!"

Laughter ran through his audience. Tayara asked the passengers to introduce themselves. It was important to him to create connections and foster openness among them. Then he took a long pause and began to speak more slowly.

"Should there be a moment of contemplation, respect the silence, it's a part of the North. Silence is an open space. It's not a void it's your soul making room so that the essential can enter it. But bear in mind that this land does not belong to you. It is we who belong to the land. Let this immensity welcome you and seduce you with the surprises it has in store for you. Well, that's enough of me talking, let's go have some of that famous tea and ban-nock."

While the tourists drank tea, the team members intro-duced themselves, including the new employees on board, Aputik among them. Along with the others, Tayara discovered the softness of her voice. He was attracted but didn't as yet know to what extent that voice would strike a chord with him.

From up on the bridge, Tayara admired the view with a few of the voyagers. The mountains, the valleys, the infinite beauty of the North. They sailed toward their first destination, the Torngat Mountains, toward Labrador. A spectacular site, one of his favourite places. Each time he visited, the same emotion overwhelmed him. In eight years, he had never tired of it, even after making four trips there every summer.

He explained to the couple, Sarah and Julien, that it was in these mountains, a very long time ago, that the shamans had met. It was an area full of spirits, a truly special place. And there were still many *nanuk*, many polar bears, there.

"Imagine, a little over a century ago, all shamanic beliefs and practises had been banished. Our culture went on without them for four generations, and then they slowly returned and ended up supplanting the religion brought by the missionaries."

"How did the shamans manage to re-establish themselves?" Sarah asked.

Tayara thought for a moment. "I'd say that renegotiating the agreement changed everything. We were coming out of the Great Sorrow, what some people also called the Great Silence. A rash of suicides had befallen our communities for at least three generations after the scandal of residential schools and colonization. Men no longer found the words. At the time, food was very expensive, we didn't have drinking water, we had little or no resources for treating the psychological distress felt in all our communities. The need to take back control of our destiny grew very quickly. After the agreements, a return to the earth became natural. This was accompanied by a reappropriation of our cultural space, including shamanism. The study of plants, beliefs, old customs. We simply put meaning back into our life. At the same time, there was great technological development implemented in the North by and for members of the Inuit community. We built our own universities and research centres. Wildlife management, the fight against global warming, agronomy, you name it. We also established community greenhouses and developed resistant vegetables that we grow for our own markets. And by the way, we have the best mushrooms in the world. We didn't eat them back in the day because they were thought to bring bad weather! And guess what we'll be eating tonight!"

"And where do you live, young man, when you're not on the boat?" asked Julien.

Just then, Aputik joined them to admire the North's famous "golden hour." When the pink and pale blue colours danced, they looked almost like the *arsaniit*, the Northern Lights.

"I live between Montreal and Puvirnituq, where I help organize the winter's cultural events at the Ikumak Museum of Inuit Art."

"So then you work with Jaakusie?" asked Aputik. "He's my roommate Manumie's cousin." Tayara turned toward her. He was already seeing the effect of the wind on her skin. Her freckles were darkening, her skin was becoming smoother than the tundra after a snowstorm. And her eyes… She looked off into the distance. He turned away as if afraid to be drawn in. And especially to keep his eyes from meeting hers.

His heart was still in Puvirnituq, with the lovely Akinisie. Exactly three years ago, Tayara had invited her to follow him to the Torngat Mountains. She was just beginning to study medicine in Puvirnituq. The city, which had developed at an incredible pace, going from a population of 2,000 to nearly 50,000 in just 20 years, was full of young students. Today, it was one biggest university centres in Canada. Young people came from all over Nunavik to study there. Since the installation of the suspension railway, designed by Inuit engineers from the University of Puvirnituq, travelling around Nunavik was child's play. You could take a train and reach any of the province's communities in less than 45 minutes.

All day long, Tayara went back over Akinisie's last words.

"I understand that you have to move, I don't see how you can be truly happy with me here. I feel like I'm an extra in your life. A stopover. I like sharing things with someone on a daily basis. It's like you always wanted something new, like you'd gotten lost in the storm. You know that deep down, I love you. But I'm starting to have feelings for someone else, someone you know. I've tried not to, but you're never here."

She took a long pause.

"It's Kalluk, right?" *Not Kalluk! Tall, handsome Kalluk, the perfect man, the hunter, the hospital's head nurse... Anyone but Kalluk!* he thought.

In his own way, Tayara was perfect, but he was also perfectly independent. He would always belong to the entire world. He was free, without ties, and that's what made him so attractive. He had mixed feelings. Jealousy, sadness. He didn't bottle them up; he had no filter. When he felt something, he felt it profoundly. How could he avoid being a little territorial? He was a child of the North, raised in its vast wilderness. Feelings were strong there, wants and desires amplified, and they echoed and growled. People lived among the animals, clinging to the natural world that reminded them daily to stay in touch with their instincts.

He enjoyed supper and was happy to be back with his colleagues, his friends, and his boss Taqqik, who was Imak Tourism's founder and was, like Tayara, from Salluit. Taqqik's two teenagers, Elaisa and Maelie, had joined the expedition. The girls were eager to sing. They were going to cover songs by Anirni, the most popular singer of the day. She had a worldwide reputation and would also be headlining the festival. This was why the girls had decided to follow their *ataata*, their father. They would be taking the train back to Kuujjuaq.

Tayara impressed the two girls by telling them that his great-grandmother had founded the festival. She had returned home after having lived much of her life far from the North, in a place of cold, grey concrete. Since then, the festival had grown along with the developing province. It had become a must-see event, drawing tens of thousands of spectators every year and featuring mainly Inuit and Indigenous artists.

He went into the main cabin. He listened to the song that his great-grandmother had popularized, an Inuktitut translation of Leonard Cohen's "Hey, That's No Way to Say

Goodbye." Aputik was singing it for the passengers. She sang it simply, in her lower register.

A powerful shiver suddenly ran through Tayara's body, a feeling much like a fever. He looked out the window. The sky was mauve. The midnight sun knew not whether it was time to rise or time to set. The mountains were black.

His old soul, borne by the experience of several generations, reminded him that he was the voyager, the translator, the bridge between people, the curious one.

Tayara was in his element.

He shed the tear that hadn't been able to fall on the cheeks of his ancestors, his *saunik*.

THE FOURTH WORLD

Isabelle Picard

Just as she did every morning, Elsie walked along the shore of the unnamed Bay. As the seasons grew ever warmer, it had carved a path up to the edge of the birch forest where, as a child, the 30-year-old woman had gone to take long walks in her snowshoes. It was a time when a pristine carpet still covered the land in winter. It must have been a dozen years since Elsie had last seen snow.

Over time, even the birch trees had changed. Once greyish white, they had gradually changed until they wore a greyish-green robe that made them appear ill. Their scent was also different. Elsie used to say that they smelled metallic.

The great cold spells of the past had also slowly given way to a permanent pre-winter, a November that stretched over four long months. Four moons, during which Elsie felt chilled to the bone as soon as she stepped outside.

That morning, she once again noticed that the water had crept up over the land. She took a deep breath and lowered her head, trying to imagine her native village, down there, all but drowned under the waves. All that was left to Elsie, the lone witness to her youth, to her roots, was this birch forest and her memories of an era she had scarcely known.

The people of her village had left long ago when the water had begun to "eat up the houses," as her grandmother used to say. They had resettled an hour's walk away, in identical little cottages devoid of colour, both literally and figuratively. Just the thought of these dwellings – which came straight out of a period of colonization and forced settlement that her people had never accepted, despite the passage of centuries – left a bitter taste in Elsie's mouth every time she imagined living there. Her house was now the forest, and never would she exchange the trees' secret for those ordered but soulless homes.

More commonly, it was Elsie who visited the people from her village. Her younger brother tried each time to convince her to move in with them, attempting to dazzle her with certain luxuries she did not have: indoor toilets, people to talk to, a bath… but she stubbornly refused. Elsie didn't mind being alone at all, as long as she felt at home. And besides, she still had the animals and the birds. At least those that hadn't disappeared. The foxes, the hares, the squirrels. A few martens. The biggest animals had died out decades earlier. First the moose, then the deer that migrated from the south. Bears hadn't been seen for years either.

The beautiful woman also had her books, which she carefully hid behind a board along the back wall. History and philosophy books in which to some extent she found her strength.

><~~><

"The Grand Neutral Council will meet tonight." Thus read the headline that played in a loop on the only news channel that the united government allowed to be broadcast in any public place. It was the network that Ilda Ivanovitch tuned in to in her humble boutique, which looked something like the general stores of yesteryear. Most of the other merchants had chosen, as a form of protest, to play music, but even that had to remain neutral. Neutrality in this specific case meant 30 carefully selected songs approved by the authorities and 50 classical pieces, the majority from a different era. Nothing that might stimulate melancholia, indignation, pride, or anger, and certainly nothing that might express individuality, a sense of belonging, or any statement of identity or culture.

The entire era of rectitude had begun with the death of Mr. Nedib the last of the humanists according to Ilda while the vultures were already circling in the corridors of the First House. They waited for ages for the President to take his last breath and then had seized power and instituted a major reform. A corrupt government proposed a modern version of a societal model that claimed to listen more attentively to the people. People who desperately needed food couldn't have cared less about protecting the planet. A population that got organized, made itself heard, and rebelled, as if the gloom of poverty and the noise of empty bellies had prevailed over past values. In reality, what this government was imposing was state-supported capitalism that enabled it to line its own pockets. "A big fat pile of rubbish," repeated Ilda. The photo of the demonstration for the Earth that she had attended 35 years earlier, hidden at the bottom of her cash register, was evidence of the battles in which she had fought during the time when limits, ceilings, carbon taxes, political correctness, and respect for others and for the planet all came to an end. It was the era of each man for himself, of conflicts between rich countries and those lacking resources.

The "bad old times," as Ilda called the period, had lasted eight long years during which the Earth kept getting warmer, the glaciers kept melting, the rich kept getting richer, and the poor kept getting weaker. The polarization of ideas spread through all social structures in a dance of the privileged, who waltzed off with everything, and the minorities, who bowed down at a dance that ended one fine morning with a total blackout of the Web. Nothing left but a great silence. Then the leaders of this world held a secret meeting, and they finally came up with a master plan: neutrality. A social project intended to re-establish peace, balance, and harmony by essentially neutralizing everything that makes us human.

The concept of neutrality was introduced into all aspects of life; it infiltrated perniciously, like a person you're eager to get to know but who turns out to be a disappointment and whose presence you ultimately regret. At nearly 70 springs, Ilda Ivanovitch had long understood that this story of great neutrality was nothing but one more of man's passing fancies that, like any movement pushed to its extremes, would eventually explode. One more movement to add to the already extensive list of the previous century's social movements and ideologies, the latest of which had contaminated everything in its path.

This "neutralism," as Ilda dubbed it, had already passed the tipping point, leaving souls grim, the land arid, and dreams impossible after years of economic wars and struggling to survive.

First came the abolition of religions, then the appearance of a single new flag for all countries that, while it had initially been flown along with territorial flags, now found itself alone at the top of the flagpole. And finally, the banning of national holidays and their replacement with the Humanity Celebration.

But it was when the language of instruction became universal and unique, a bit like George Orwell's Newspeak, that Ilda withdrew from the great plan. An ambitious plan, for sure, one that certain people hurried to describe as the biggest mistake in the history of humanity. They staged a flurry of demonstrations, each one more raucous than the next, that the forces of neutral officers then practically suppressed out of existence. Philosophers, anthropologists, sociologists, historians, political scientists, and all of the movement's dissenters – thousands of people – were erased, disappeared from the face of the planet in a series of arrests justified by the conformity required for the survival of the human race. Then little by little, the people became resigned, driven by fear or too busy trying to survive.

Ilda had lost many clients since the beginning of the Great Shift to Neutrality. She managed, thanks to the government assistance offered to those who agreed to cooperate and comply to "see the light." Ilda consoled herself, telling herself that she was the only one in the region who had an organic cricket farm. Her flour was the finest and the richest in proteins for miles around, and it was certainly the least expensive. This is how the imposing, six-foot-tall woman managed to get by month after month. It was also due to the reduced prices at which she offered her products, even in small quantities, a certain advantage conferred by her half-hearted alliance with the government.

Every time the Grand Neutral Council met, restrictions were tightened. With each Great Announcement, Ilda felt she was losing a piece of herself, or rather that she had to bury fragments of her humanity in her secret garden, where no light of day would ever find them, sometimes losing them in the process.

><

As she did twice a month, Elsie went to the village. The old Russian lady's store was the one she preferred. The price of groceries had something to do with this choice, but she especially liked the odd woman who, with her strong accent, reminded her of a time when the music of different cultures could be heard everywhere. It was if she got a little taste of travel whenever they met.

Elsie liked to imagine the old lady's life, and each time she visited, she added a little something to the story that she was inventing and that was becoming more and more like a Kafka novel, the mood of the times being a contributing factor, no doubt.

As Elsie roamed around the flour section, two neutral officers came in, ringing the bell hanging on the door. Dressed in grey, the men approached the counter where the Russian woman was sitting. Elsie, immobile behind the shelves of cricket flour, watched the scene unfold.

"Hello. We've been told that you have things in your possession that are not culturally neutral. We insist that you give them to us immediately."

"No, nothing of the sort. I am a friend of the regime. Look at my screen…"

The silver-haired lady pointed a finger at the television, which was airing the same three news stations authorized by the government.

"Madam, you would not be the first to…"

"Madam, your items, please," ordered the taller of the two, who was clearly growing impatient.

"I have a customer," replied the shop owner, raising her head and indicating with her chin.

"We will watch her. We're waiting for you. You know the consequences."

"But I'm telling you, I have nothing. I burned every-thing, as we were told to do."

"Get going!" yelled the shorter man, indicating the door leading into the house.

Elsie, jaw clenched, was silent. She knew there was no way out of the situation. If Mrs. Ivanovitch went in search of something reminiscent of anything from her past, from her native Russia, she risked having her store closed, and if she didn't obey, things would end exactly the same way.

Elsie walked toward the two men, dragging her leather boots along the floor. The officers turned toward her.

"Hey, you, aren't you that Savage who wants to remain savage? You are forbidden to wear moccasins."

"These aren't moccasins, they're soft boots."

"Just who do you take us for? You, you're not allowed to wear those."

"*Especially* you," added the tall one, tapping his finger on Mrs. Ivanovitch's counter. "We're going to burn those moccasins for you. Take them off! Now!"

This was the second time neutral officers had had seized Elsie's mukluks. She did as she was told. She would just make more, as many times as took.

Smirking, the man grabbed the boots off the floor and put then in a bag.

"You are lucky, ma'am," he said as he turned toward the shopkeeper, who had frozen in place as she witnessed the interaction. "We'll leave with this, but the next time someone denounces you, we won't be so nice. We'll search for ourselves, and we'd better not find anything. So you know what to do."

The two officers exited. Ilda left her cash register and went over to the shoe rack, gesturing to Elsie to follow. The shopkeeper moved a few boxes before being satisfied and opening one.

"Size nine, right? This is for you!" said Ilda, offering Elsie a pair of new brown boots.

"I can't accept, ma'am. I live in the woods. I'll just ruin them, and you won't be able to resell them."

"They are yours. You got me out of a terrible jam. You deserve them. You have a good heart," added the woman with the characteristic accent that betrayed her origins.

Elsie smiled at her, then pursed her lips the way she did every time she got an idea.

"Here's what I suggest. Loan me some old boots for as long as it takes me to make new mukluks, and I'll bring them back next time I visit. In any case, new boots that are too stiff will hurt my feet."

"But… how can I thank you then? What if I invite you to have supper with me?" the woman asked, with a wide smile.

"I would never say no to a good supper, but I have to go check my traps before nightfall. How would tomorrow be?"

"Tomorrow is perfect," replied Ilda, emphasizing the *r* sound.

"I'll bring bannock made with your flour."

"Bannock?" asked the sexagenarian, with a frown.

"It's a bread from home. Well, not really from home, but I'll explain…"

"And I'll make solyanka soup and a bird's milk. They can't very well come and question what's on our plates."

"Ah, that…"

Uncertain of the ground she was walking on, Elsie said no more, showing a judiciousness that she had learned to develop, like a reflex. After paying for a few purchases, the young woman put on her winter hat and went out the door, ringing the bell again as she left.

～～

Night had already fallen by the time Elsie arrived at Mrs. Ivanovitch's the next day. The woman, who had heard Elsie's old four-wheeler, was waiting at the door to her house, next to her shop.

"Welcome! Come in!"

Elsie gave Ilda a parcel wrapped in a piece of fabric while she awkwardly tried to take off the brown boots. The harder she pulled, the more difficult the manoeuvre became, and although she tried to do it gracefully and courteously, she fell with her shoulder against the wall, sending both women into gales of laughter.

"I'm so happy you're here. I don't often have visitors," said the silver-haired woman as she hung Elsie's coat on a hanger.

"And aside from my family and more rarely, a few people from my village, I don't see many people either. Especially since…"

As she had the day before, Elsie stopped. Ilda, who had understood her fear, added, "You know, I'm older than you. I've seen things… I've heard things too…"

But Elsie changed the subject.

"Your home is lovely. It's big. Do you live alone?" she asked, despite knowing the answer.

"I have two sons, but they moved to Greenville a long time ago. One of them is an engineer," she stated proudly.

"An engineer… wow! There must be plenty of work with all the rebuilding that has to be done. And the other?"

The shopkeeper's face tensed a bit and lost its glow.

"The other one I haven't heard from in three years. Just one letter saying not to worry, that he was fine. Unsigned. Not even in his handwriting."

"Oh… I'm sorry. But at least he's okay…" Elsie tried to reassure the mother, who took a moment to react.

"Well! That's not the whole story, you know. I don't even know your name! Mine is Ilda Ivanovitch."

"And mine is Elsie Brascoupé," she relied, extending her hand.

"Delighted, Elsie! Come, have a seat."

Ilda pointed to a well-laid table, little plates on top of the big ones, in a fashion Elsie hadn't seen in a very long time. The young woman chose the seat close to the wall.

"Do you drink wine?

"Yes, with pleasure," said Elsie, smiling.

While Ilda served the wine, Elsie looked around. The wall in front of her was covered with framed photographs of unfamiliar landscapes. She thought that they must be places in Russia. Then she noticed the Ponte Vecchio in Florence and above it, a black sand beach, and the Arc de Triomphe just below.

"Did you take these pictures? Impressive! You've been to quite a few countries…"

"Yes. When I was young, when I left Russia. Before coming here, I lived in Paris for a few years and then in Italy. But over there, in Europe, it was hard for us foreigners. At a certain point, I no longer felt safe so I came to Canada. At least what was called Canada at the time. I've been living her for 37 years now. How about you?"

"Me? I was born very near here. I grew up here and have travelled very little."

"You're young. It's not easy to travel anymore, not these days, and that's a shame."

"But at the same time…"

Taken aback, Elsie stopped again.

Understanding her discomfort, which she shared because nothing was private and everything could be reported to the neutral officers, Ilda hastened to start over.

"So tonight, I've made you some recipes from my country: a solyanka soup and a bird's milk, a cake that's called *ptichye moloko* in Russian. Have you had it?"

"Ah! That's what bird's milk is… I was wondering," said Elsie, blushing, no doubt due to the glass of wine she'd just swallowed in almost one gulp.

"You know, Elsie, I see you in my shop twice a month. I watch you, but I know nothing about you. You're not like the others. What I mean is…"

Elsie understood well what Ilda was trying to say. It was true. She was not like the other members of her clan. She'd always thought she'd been born in the wrong era, as if she belonged to a different century. Despite that, she was secretly content to be living at this very moment, perhaps because to a certain extent, she believed that, in her own way, she would help change things.

The young woman's way of life was already different, as if she were torn between the 20th and the 21st centuries. Most of the time, Elsie was alone. Of course, she went to the hamlet to see her family and her nieces and nephews as often as possible, but she liked to be in the woods, at least in what remained of them, in the little hut that served as a refuge, where only the solar panels and the wood-burning stove provided the energy she needed on the coldest days.

Ilda reopened the conversation, asking, "What do you do for a living?"

"I sell meat and skins when I can. I don't need all that much. I saved the money that the government gave us before wiping us off the map for good, and I dip into that only if necessary. You understand… it's not much, but it's enough. Tomorrow, who can say? I'll see. I studied computer science, but…"

Elsie wondered if Ilda did understand. Ilda felt her doubt and put her hands on Elsie's, smiling at her as a mother would. From that moment on, Elsie knew that she was on friendly territory and would no longer have to censor herself.

"That's not terribly useful these days, eh?" added Ilda, finishing Elsie's sentence.

"No, not so much."

The evening flowed smoothly. The food was delicious, and the bannock and red-berry jam that Elsie had brought perfectly complemented the meal. The young woman let herself be lulled by Ilda's stories, which took her from Russia to the Italian countryside as well as to Paris, Toulouse, and Vienna.

Seeing that the woman was somewhat tipsy from the wine and because it was late, Elsie suggested that she herself serve the bird's milk. While looking for a knife in one of the drawers, she came upon the letter from Ilda's son, who revealed only a few details, just as Ilda had said. It was an unsigned typescript that said he was doing well. And at the very bottom right, a minuscule stain could barely be seen. Making sure that her hostess wasn't watching her, Elsie brought the letter closer to her face. The dot at the bottom of the missive was in fact a tiny blue star, a symbol that she recognized. Her instincts hadn't been wrong. She returned the letter to the drawer, asking Ilda for a hint as to where to find the big knives and then cutting two large portions of the appetizing cake.

"Have you noticed those blue stars all over the city?" Elsie asked as she brought the plates to the table.

"I've seen a few, yes. There was even one on my door last month. All that paint that I had to scrape off... It's rebels, I think. But they should be careful, or they'll end up like the others."

"You think there's nothing the people can do about it? About what's happening, I mean."

"They tried, you know. Maybe you were too young..."

"No, I'm 30! I remember everything. My mother... my uncle... my older brother..."

Elsie stopped, her eyes full of tears.

"I'm so sorry, my dear. Those were terrible times..." said Ilda, putting her hand on the forearm of her guest, who quickly got hold of herself, a spark of anger in her eyes.

"Then there's also the story of the Six. Have you heard of it, Ilda?"

"Nothing but a legend! It's been what? Three years that people have been talking about it? Where are they? How did they help us, eh? Six people who would save everyone? Come on!" she replied, pouring herself some more wine.

"They're getting ready, I'm sure... It doesn't happen just by snapping your fingers," said Elsie.

"So in your opinion, the stars have something to do with all that? With the Six?"

"That's what I'm hearing," said Elsie with a sly smile.

"But..."

"And there's the Hopi legend too," interrupted Elsie, a twinkle in her eye.

"Ah! Let me hear it..." Ilda said in her typical accent, with the stressed *r* sound.

"It's an old story. The Hopi people believe that the world has already been created and destroyed three times. According to them, the appearance of a blue star signals the end of this, the fourth world.

"There are two ways to understand this legend: either our world is going to be destroyed or it will be reborn differently."

"Me, I'd vote for the second conclusion, dear girl!" exclaimed Ilda, who was getting more and more inebriated.

"Me, too, Ilda, me too. I have a feeling that something is in the works. I'm just thinking out loud here, but those graffiti stars give me hope. You have to see the signs," said Elsie, gazing at the woman.

At last, the young woman rose, thanked her hostess, and went to the door, where she put on her coat and somewhat more easily pulled on the used boots the woman had loaned her. Ilda followed her with a piece of bird's milk that she'd wrapped up. When she lifted her long thick hair to free it from her fitted coat, Elsie revealed the inconspicuous tattoo of a little blue star on her neck. Ilda understood and smiled. Elsie opened the heavy door.

"Look, Ilda! It's snowing!"

"You've done wonders for me, Elsie. Come back whenever you like," said the old woman as she studied the sky, still shocked by the connection she had just made.

"I'll come back. I promise."

"Don't forget your cake!" exclaimed the woman.

As she was returning home, Elsie made a quick stop at a modest shack that looked like an outhouse, or at best, like a shed lost among the forest's birch trees. She entered and knocked three times on the inside wall, using a specific rhythm. A door opened, and Elsie went down the stairway, still holding the *ptichye moloko*. She gave the cake to a very tall man in his 30s who was sitting at a wall of computer screens and wires. A man who, if you listened carefully, spoke with traces of a Russian accent, and rolled his *r*'s. She smiled at him as she tenderly put her hand on his.

Then she said, "Your mother's doing well."

SAUSAGES

J.D. Kurtness

On the menu this morning, eight very fresh sausages. Three big fancy ones to pick up at the Amap, then five unsavoury ones to extract from the governmental quagmire. I prefer to work alone, but today is Monday. The company no longer offers weekend pickups; anyone who croaked since last Friday night is waiting for us. I took my dose of painkillers, antidepressants, and stimulants, well-mixed into a fluorescent green, watermelon-flavoured protein drink. I'm ready.

Théo is here to help me. He's dozing on the passenger side, his chin wet with drool. I like Théo a lot. He's always in a good mood, and he does everything I ask of him. His only vice is soft drinks. He ingests two litres of Pepsi a day. He's the only Down's syndrome person I know. Parents normally opt for an abortion when they learn their child will be "developmentally delayed," but his folks were believers. Before they died, they entrusted him to the company. It takes good care of him. I watch him sleeping as we move along. The pickup truck knows the way. Twenty minutes, and we see the Amap Hotel up ahead, in the middle of a sea of asphalt and barbwire fences. I wake Théo up; our lovely eyes must be scanned before we can enter the enormous building.

A spanking clean dolly awaits us in the hall. Our sausages' contact info is written on a laminated card placed on top if it. I count four lines instead of three. So we have an extra sausage, still warm, to transport this morning.

We are given a waterproof suit and boots and gloves made of very stiff rubber. Nothing like the soft, worn out equipment we have to wear when we go remove dead beneficiaries from their public compartments. Here, where it's private, the sausages get their money's worth. And it doesn't smell so bad either. My gagging is just a reflex. Any odour even vaguely resembling that of a solute sets it off. I get nauseated in the dairy section of the supermarket and the cold storage rooms of convenience stores. A pile of boxes left out in the rain can almost make me puke. In May, I avoid certain roads because they're bordered by wildflowers whose heady perfume reminds me of that grey-beige pulp.

The day's first sausage is a woman named Teasdale, Amélie: 64 years old, 69 kilograms of greasy meat. She's easy to spot, the only unit glowing red in the long, blue-tinted corridor. According to the capsule's screen, her heart stopped beating on Saturday afternoon at 2:38. I was taking a nap when she died. Théo? Théo doesn't know what he was doing. I hold the dolly while my colleague hauls Amélie Teasdale out by her feet. The suction noise makes him smile; I see his eyes crinkle under his visor. We pull out the tubes, disconnect the catheters and electrodes, we extubate the body, which is cold. The system detects the dead ones and automatically cools down their compartment. A map offers top-quality service, funeral in the other world included. All the avatars are decked out in their best clothes for the occasion. I saw pictures in an advertisement. I mop up most of the solute to keep it from dripping every-where. Théo is in fine form this morning; he lifts the corpse without waiting for assistance from the lift mechanism. I slide the body bag underneath, and we zip it up. We role Amélie to the pickup truck, and then we repeat the process with the three remaining sausages.

⤛〰⤜

The government building seems pathetic in comparison to its competition. The smell reaches us from the far end of the parking lot. My legs hurt so I park the pickup near the entrance, despite my revulsion. I swallow a little mouthful of watermelon to buck up my courage before getting out of the vehicle.

While the machine verified our access cards, the civil servant – a certain Pierre, according to the badge pinned to his shirt – eyeballed Théo. Everyone stares at Théo when they meet him for the first time. We put on our own gear. The dolly's metal wheels squeak. We leave it near the elevator on the fifth floor, where the wheels get stuck in the grated floor. A rail system supporting a stainless-steel stretcher pulled by a winch is used to transport the bodies. The smell is pestilential. All the residents of single a floor bathe in the same juice. The bodies' sporadic movements spatter the floor with slimy solute, hence the grillwork. The designers took their inspiration from slaughterhouses. It's hot, and no light is emitted except for that coming from the bulbs mounted on our visors and from the backlighting emitted by monitors above the units.

Bouliane, Keven: 46 years old, lies in a slurry of urine and fecal matter. His 126 kilos are too much to lift, even for Théo. The hoist is broken, so we have to improvise. I detach the chain from the stretcher on rails and pass it through the useless device's pulley before wrapping it around Keven's pale, hairy ankles. The skin peels off when I activate the winch; the body is not the least bit fresh. The body rises slowly. It hangs by the ankles, limp and shiny, above the hallway. I'm dripping with sweat and feel ill. For a brief moment, I hope to take my turn in the other world, to connect to the matrix to find the others. Théo wraps his arms around me. He gently clasps me against his rubber suit. He's crying too. We sniffle, finish the task, and collect ourselves before going back past civil servant Pierre with our cargo.

We go back for the four others. The dead here are so young, younger than the ones we collected from the private establishment. Here, minimal conditions for survival are assured, but nothing more. The food is inferior, the solute, common. In the early years, people were lying on beds, like in a hospital. There weren't enough employees to turn them over. Employees managed to transmit images of bedsores from the other side. Even though reality no longer interests the majority of people, some are concerned enough to force the government to soak those in their charge in solute, as it's done in the private sector. The solute's quality is, however, mediocre. I suspect that the drought is currently aggravating the problem. Twenty-six straight days without rain has made the price of water skyrocket. Théo and I are rationed; the company allows each of us one litre a day, and the rest we have to pay for ourselves. No one, aside from undertakers like us, is aware of the changed density of the public marinade, which is filtered too slowly. In any case, the scandal would never break today. Reality no longer has a place in anyone's thoughts.

In public establishments, people are never disconnected. That's a promise, cross my heart and hope to die. It's written into the law, on both sides of reality. One can't say the same for the private giants' servers. Certain individuals spend all their money in the other world and then can no longer pay for their accommodations. Then it's eviction time. I do that in the afternoon, after taking the sausages to the incinerator and getting Théo back to the company's dormitory.

⤛⤜

Two protein bars, seven sugary mouthfuls, and I'm on the attack. I don't know what Lepage, Aube: 24 years old, 37 kilos, did to deserve this. But I can imagine. The tales of eviction are all horribly similar. I'm on the third floor of the immense Gosoft Complex. At least as alone as you can be with thousands of wired-up people busy having fabulous adventures. A more zealous than average employee might even be watching me do it on the images relayed by the security cameras. Torment is a disheartening spectacle, but a spectacle nonetheless. The young woman's skin appears translucent. I identify the network of veins that irrigates her atrophied muscles. I work gently, respectfully. I pull out the probes, catheters, and tubes. I wash the body as best I can before the fateful moment. I take a deep breath and disconnect the electrodes. Three seconds pass. Then Aube opens her eyes and screams, the hoarse sound of a terrified animal. I prefer this to the catatonics you have to carry, and even more to the silent ones who tear at their wrists with their long, filthy nails so they can bleed to death and stop their suffering.

It doesn't last long; the disconnected person's voice breaks after a few seconds. The others aren't aware of anything. Their involuntary movements make a slight slapping sound. The peaceful atmosphere contrasts with my sausage's distress. I offer her some water, but she pushes my hand away and tries to reconnect the electrodes. I restrain her easily. Years of inertia make her no match against my outcast's body, no matter how tired it is. I sing a lullaby. Aube calms down, grows still. I help her put on the pale clothing and soft shoes. She can get up and walk if I support her. We leave the floor. The more quickly we leave, the easier the transition will be. Fortunately, the compartments are closed. Aube cannot see the blissful faces.

When we get back to the pickup, I offer her 125 millilitres of fruit juice, the last item she is entitled to with her package deal. She is floating in the shapeless Gosoft clothes. I explain that I am taking her back to my employer. Several options are available to people in her situation. She can stay to regain her strength, and every day of lodging will cost her one week of work. She is free to leave when she wants, provided that she repays her lodging debt by working. She can work in the fields, the solute factory, the mines, or even do what I do and deal with sausages. Obviously, I don't call them that in front of her. I use the word "clients."

"Can you turn down the lights?" I raise my head toward the top of the passenger cab. It's closed; the client doesn't want the daylight to be so bright. That one's too much for me, and I burst out laughing. A pout appears, and her lips begin to tremble. She's crying. I'm already tired of hearing her, so I loan her my sunglasses. "This place sucks!"

She's not wrong. I start the truck. During the hour-long trip, I learn that Aube had been connected since she was a very young child. She and her parents made the leap together. She has no idea where they are now; she quickly lost sight of them in the other world. She admits that she hasn't thought about them since she was a teenager. Aube has three children. She speaks of them with pride, as if they actually existed. Yet she has spent the last 15 years in a stainless-steel tube where the only human contact is the annual baseline neurological functions exam. Waking the subject is not required for this test.

My passenger watches the landscape go by. The sun is blazing, and we feel the heat despite the ever-present shadows created by the clouds of dust. She drank all of the fruit juice. I advise her to pay attention to her sphincters. I don't want to insult her, but there's a risk of relaxation and release after spending 15 years unconcerned about biological functions. I'd forgotten the diapers.

After a few minutes of silence, Aube asks me why I'm here. I detect a certain scorn in her voice, the newly ejected person's typical attitude toward those they think were subjected to the same fate as they. Losers have no use for each other. Does she think I ruined my life by buying too many outfits made of multicoloured pixels? The shock can be read all over her face. I reassure her; I'm not a clairvoyant, and there hasn't been any violation of confidentiality. Her story is banal, nothing more. The evicted have all been kicked out for what I consider to be more or less absurd reasons. I've disconnected hundreds like her, and those who can speak sometimes tell me how they ended up spending all their money for virtual possessions whose relevance I struggle to understand: highly developed avatars, time spent with celebrities (the celebrity in question being present in the form of his or her avatar), personalized microclimates, fantastic animals to enhance an artificial menagerie, and so on. The embellishments recur in these stories of ruin.

I'm here voluntarily. My response horrifies the young woman.

"But how can people live like this? In this non-existence? We've been driving for half an hour and nothing is happening. Your face is wrinkled, and your skin is covered with spots. And what is that disgusting stench?"

The odour is her own. Aube has been coated with an antibiotic lubricant for more than a decade. She also needs to see a dentist. I refuse to put any music on. I know, it's dangerous; my passenger might start to wonder about things if she's left alone with her thoughts, but I'm willing to run the risk. I open the window, and fresh air fills the passenger compartment. The smell of the wind, the light, the rare birds heard in summer – that's why I stay here. I don't want to give all that up.

"But there, you have all the sounds, all the landscapes, and all the smells you want. It's better, so much better… I think I'm going to be sick."

Aube gagged on the side of the road but didn't vomit anything up. I give her three weeks before we find her hanging in the company dormitory or drowned in the river. Life has no value for her, and she has no chance of returning to her virtual life, the only one that she deems worth living. She will realize this very soon. ·

I take her to the office where they register the newly evicted. I am no longer responsible. My workday is done.

My apartment is small and dark. It's all I can afford on my salary and its numerous deductions. I act tough in front of the clients, but my moments of weakness are growing more frequent. I picture myself joining the never-ending party with the rest of the imbeciles. Never coming back. Entrusting, for the years remaining to me, my corporeal self to bored employees until some poor sod pulls me out by the feet and sends me to the incinerator. I'd have to go public since I don't have the money to pay for a more luxurious capsule. But I have doubts about my ability to forget that I'm marinating in other people's shit. And I'd still have to save quite a pile of money just to be hosted on the government server. The system is designed so that all our savings are used up. A sort of final tax. It's the scheme the government devised for taxing those who choose the other side. The private companies' servers are beyond our borders. The money has migrated to this cybernetic no man's land designed to suck up money and fry our brains. Only the nostalgic and the impoverished folks who work in this concrete world still pay taxes. The system is dying.

The worst is that even if you have a paying job in this artificial construct, you end up spending all your money, like the client I had this afternoon. But she's right. I lead a mediocre life. I plod along, completing gruesome tasks. I gorge on little pills to compensate for the lack of human contact. If I were younger and prettier, I would have taken my chances on the idyllic islands, home to those who have it all. Private estates where the self-sufficient privileged live. People for whom the world is so marvellous that they never, ever thought of hooking up their own machine.

There are a few hundred thousand of us who take care of the millions of people who are wired up. No one left to worry about us. Laws, money, happiness, and preoccupations are now in a universe that we cannot access. Devastation, floods, fires, nothing matters around here anymore. Services are minimal; we are but dust, a nuisance, an unpleasant afterthought. No one wants to hear about us, or the planet, or the quality of the water, the air, the soil, or the food we eat or put into our stomach with a feeding tube. Their world eliminated suffering, guilt, and uncertainty. That's what they claim in their ubiquitous advertisements.

The sun has irradiated my skin, the dark pigments gain a little more territory each day. My joints hurt, and cataracts cloud my eyes. I should have worn tinted glasses earlier on. Hospitals are expensive, and when people like me go in, they never come out. I couldn't pay for treatment. Even if I could, I'd have to go back a few months later for a new lump, a new pain, a new problem caused by the pollution in which I've always bathed. The rare children who are born are smaller and more anxious, learn more slowly. Except those born to the rich: those children, it seems, are veritable geniuses and are physically fit. They eat healthy, balanced meals, live in villas topped by a dome that filters out harmful rays and allows in those that help synthesize vitamin D. Those families hop from one island to the next in a private jet. Sometimes they even go into outer space. They're seeking a new planet to colonize because this one has almost nothing left to offer them. They may have already left, and we maintain these death wards, hoping that we'll be able to bed down in one, too.

Tuesday: three sausages to incinerate and two disconnections. Wednesday: five sausages, three disconnections. Thursday, a pump broke down: 18 sausages. Dehydration was fatal for the weakest. We didn't do any disconnections that day. Not the next day either, with 39 sausages to cook. Monday, there were 140 names written on the laminated card. Two crazy weeks of piling up body bags, then a whole week of disconnections, one after the other. One sausage tried to poke my eye out. I needed a shot of Toradol to get me through the rest of the day.

This morning, I can't take it anymore, I just can't get up. I have my telephone near me. All I have to do is tap three times, and the money is transferred. My entire life savings. They come to get me.

It's Théo and Aube. The injection is painful, I'm surprised, but very quickly I relax.

KANATABE ISHKUEU

Natasha Kanapé Fontaine

During the 2020s, new technologies were introduced to the world or were vastly improved. Humanity witnessed the robotization of many aspects of daily life. Changes in the planet's way of life occurred more quickly, and an increasing number of robots were helping humans. By 2033, there was almost one robot per inhabitant of the planet. Permanently connected to the Web, they specifically contributed to the democratization of knowledge; education would never again be commodified since an international decree abolished tuition fees around the world. Education would thereafter be financed by the United Nations, which made its profits from cryptocurrency. Each robot helped circulate data and human knowledge, ensuring that no one was left without knowledge, past or present.

In 2035, it was announced that even though technology had repeatedly been able to delay it, global warming would ultimately cause an unexpected setback in the climate situation over the next 20 years: the return of the ice age.

For 20 years, Kanatabe had drawn on the ancestral knowledge of its territory's Indigenous peoples and built a great number of giant infrastructures above cities and urban centres so that the snow and extreme cold would not disturb the lives of humans or of any other living things.

The African countries, a world power ever since their inhabitants had wrested control of their natural resources from Europe and China, followed the Kanatabe model and developed strategies to save tropical vegetation. Kanatabe became their first partner in the development and expansion of this "climate architecture," as it would come to be called around the globe.

This new ice age began around 2048, and by 2054, it had fully taken hold.

❦

I open my eyes, and I don't recognize where I am right away. Everything is blurry. My right hand is on my stomach. When I wiggle my fingers, I feel the texture of a wool blanket. I wonder if it's real wool. I somehow manage to turn onto my right side. My left hand joins my right on my stomach. I bend my head toward my knees, and I get up. Finally, I'm curled into a little ball on what appears to be the ground. I close my eyes again. They hurt; they're dry. Opening them back up is difficult. So I go back to sleep in that position.

I doze for a few moments, then try opening my eyes again. I'm seeing better. I glance around me. I detect walls. I notice rays of light behind a brown surface. A blanket has been hung to create a curtained entry. I don't hear anything. A breeze moves the panel of fabric that serves as a door. I feel the air reach me, caress my uncovered forehead. I lower my lids. The breeze had slipped into my brain through my pupils, its crispness instantly filling my head. It travels down the length of my neck and expands my chest.

I release a long sigh. I still don't know where I am. I'm not sure I really want to know.

As I inhale again, I roll back onto my back, and after rubbing my eyes, I begin to study the ceiling. It appears to be made of wood, such a rare commodity these days. Long slender tree branches seem to form a somewhat hexagonal structure, rising above another one, made of the same kind of branches, on which it is resting. All the intersections are bound together and covered with what looks to be dried animal sinews, an ancient method, an almost forgotten method, but one that perfectly insulates a dwelling like this.

And this coverlet? I touch the fabric I'm lying on. It's warm and soft. What is this wool? The furthest back I can remember is synthetic wool, but then our clothes began to be designed and manufactured to be as thin as possible, while still being warm enough to wear during the ice age we had entered some 50 years earlier. We don't really wear synthetic wool anymore. It's sometimes used for tapestries or wall decorations, like an artefact whose use has been forgotten.

Since the structure I'm in is made of natural materials, I suspect that this wool comes from an animal. Except that animal wool hasn't been held by human hands for decades… especially not my people's hands. If I remember correctly, I heard talk of muskoxen from north of the Canadian Shield. Global warming melted the permafrost and raised temperatures north of the 55th parallel, the result being that the population of these muskoxen, which were quite rare in the 2020s, grew and that some herds migrated westward. The caribou and the moose, if I have their names right, had basically disappeared, so my people began to eat muskoxen. Because the roads had been closed, they used snowmobiles to go hunting on the great expanses and between the hills of the Canadian Shield.

My memory is coming back slowly; everything else remains fuzzy. A headache is building behind my eyeballs. I close my eyes again. I rub my palms across my eyelids, then on my forehead and temples. I'd like to feel that little breeze once again, the one that came through here a moment ago.

Muskox. It seems so familiar… I have a vague memory of my *mushum* walking in a tent. I feel the breeze. Ah, it's so refreshing! I breathe it in. Then I bury my nose in the wool on my makeshift bed, and I see tree branches and green needles on the ground. I seem to be lying on a mattress of twigs. It's comfortable. I inhale the wool's scent; it smells of fire. I move a little as I stretch; I inhale once again. I know this tree. It lives in my memory.

I see my grandfather again, bustling about the tent. I'm very little. He's humming something. He turns to me and offers me some food. I take it in my hand. I recognized the smell. A bird. It's a strong, intense taste. I loved it as a child. I hear a word in the mist: *ple-u*. It's a bird that no longer exists. It's grey with black spots. It's cold outside. I notice the sound of the wind. Voices echoing outdoors. They're calling my *mushum*. He goes to the door, puts on his boots, pants, and coat. Then a fur hat. Fur… He goes out, and I hear people talking loudly. Laughing heartily. Everyone is joking around, a few voices, words that I don't catch, and again everyone bursts out laughing. Peaceful voices. Happy laughter. The scent of snow reaches me. I devoured that piece of meat. It was juicy. My *mushum* comes back inside the tent, carrying fir boughs in his arms.

I slept on a bed of fir! Where could I be? Despite my heavy head, I sit up on the pallet. I realize that I'm not wearing my own clothes. Then I remember. Someone carried me here. I was exhausted. Yes, someone found me outside, and I was brought to this encampment.

I had been looking for this place! I made it here! I take my feet out from under the blanket, remove my soft little shoes, and check the condition of my toes. They're a bit blue, but that's alright. My fingers aren't red. I could have gotten frostbite. I walked in the snow for a long time, until a storm caught up to me, and the winds eventually reduced visibility. I couldn't see anything anymore.

I lie back down. My headache is getting worse. There must be people outside, but I'm too exhausted to get up. I dreamt so often about this place! I'd heard talk of it for at least 30 years, but no map could help us find this clan, which lives in seclusion on Nitassinan territory.

Tears fall from my eyes. My people's elders told us so many things about the hidden clan and about their houses made of wood, tree branches, and bark; about their roofs covered with furs and thick skins; about their clothing made of the same materials. When people heard this story, they made jokes about it. It was like a slightly foolish legend told to make children dream. Who, in the 2100s, would still live that way, considering everything that technology can do for us?

Artificial intelligence has made us omniscient. And especially during this ice age, everything that could have been invented *was* invented to keep us warm and healthy and to reassure us – this ice age will last only one more century. Of course, a large number of us will not live to see it come to an end, but we understand that it's not eternal. Scientists from all over the world, human and artificial, are working tirelessly to try to shorten it. Except that the ice is powerful. The snow – which, incidentally, had practically disappeared in the 2030s – is powerful. Mother Earth is powerful. My people, the Innuat, believe that She gave us technology to help us, to help herself as well, all out of love, but never in a million years were we to use it in an attempt to dominate or control her actions. Nevertheless, technology didn't help us save our mother tongue, Innu-aimun. We haven't spoken it for 50 years now.

And here I am, lying on a bed of fir boughs. It was made with a technique that I thought had vanished because trees couldn't survive the worsening drought of the 2020s. Fir trees were literally wiped off the map of Keb during the huge forest fires of 2029, which were worse than the Australian fires of 2019, and were replaced by deciduous trees a few years later.

Keb was once a province called Quebec and is today a free state within the United States of Kanatabe. Canada and Quebec, like other nations around the world, were renamed, either by reclaiming a name from one of the territory's Indigenous languages or returning to the root of their name. Kanatabe (*Kanata-Ahbee*) means "land of many villages." Keb comes from de Kebeq, meaning "where the river narrows," and refers to the capital, Québec City.

I've heard that in Quebec, the fir tree was a valiant warrior fighting numerous ills. It would have been utterly essential, considering the great cold that shrouded the entire Earth. It exists elsewhere but would be accessible only in the form of special products, regulated by some country or other – I no longer know which one. And the few protected areas still remaining are fiercely guarded by the World Nations' national security.

I lean toward the ground to smell the branches. Their aroma is strong and awakens my memory. My tears start to fall in earnest.

I hear steps outside. I sit down with difficulty, clutching to me the precious blanket made of muskox wool, and I wait for someone to appear at the cabin's entrance.

A face slips inside. A gentle face with high cheekbones and skin the colour of wood. A smile forms on his lips. He comes in.

"*Kuei…*"

His voice is as gentle as his face.

"Uh… hi…"

He chuckles. "I just said hello to you! You answered correctly, so don't worry about that. So tell me, how do you feel?"

"Uh… I have a bit of a headache, but I'm okay."

"Okay, wait, I have something for you…"

He goes over to a raised board that serves as a counter. It holds some Mason jars, a few porcelain cups, and a contraption with two metal rings. It looks like a camp stove. I feel as if I've gone one hundred years back in time. I've seen only images from those days: photographs of families, our ancestors, who went into the woods, when the woods still existed, and camped there. I recognize these objects, which I've seen in e-books. I must be dreaming.

The man picks up a cup and an old-fashioned teapot. On the tiny stove, something is boiling in a pot. Holding a towel, he uses both hands to lift it and pours the contents into the cup. After placing the pot back on the burner, he opens a Mason jar that appears to contain a blend of herbs. The man takes a fairly big pinch of it and puts it in the cup. He stirs it with a spoon and then comes back over to me. He moves forward slowly, bends down close to my little bed, and hands me the cup.

"Careful, it's hot… The herbs are local, they'll help get you back on your feet."

"Thanks."

He watches me sympathetically as I bring the cup to my lips and take a sip. The liquid tastes delicious, and as I swallow the tea, I immediately feel the brew's freshness alter something in my body. I quickly take another sip. And then another. It does me a world of good.

"I don't want to take up too much of your time or your energy. You just got here, and you're in pretty bad shape. Get some rest. I've just got one question that's been bothering me since you showed up out of nowhere.

"Hmm… go ahead…"

"How'd you do it?"

He was quiet for a moment. Like a breath held.

"Do what?"

He stared at me questioningly.

"Find us?"

I see his eyes follow the shape of my eyebrows, my eyes, my cheeks.

"What?"

I return his surprised look.

"Well, exactly how *did* you find us? How could you have walked all the way here?"

Caught off guard, I ask myself the very same question. Time suddenly seems to stand still. We share a moment of surprise mixed with wariness. I decide to ask another question in response to his. I've just discovered where they've been hiding for a century, convincing me that there must have been three generations living there.

"Are the elders who first arrived here still alive?"

He observes me for a moment before replying.

"No, several years have already passed since they left us. But we ensured the transfer of knowledge. I can take you to speak to Atenaru, the elder who received teachings from the greatest number of elders possible."

"A great number? How many of them were there?"

"Hey, whoa! First, tell me your name! Before going on with this conversation, I have to get to know you! How do I know you're not spying for the government?"

"Who do you think you are, talking to me like that? You should trust me! I've spent my whole life searching for this place!"

"But how are we to know? You showed up here, you were dazed, we were very worried about you. Even though you were wearing clothes made for the extreme cold, you seemed frozen and couldn't speak. No one from the outside world has ever made it here, not since our grandparents arrived! Never! So who would be persistent enough to find us, other than the search officers authorized to retrieve any dissident they find?"

"The government of Kanatabe would never do that."

"What? You think you know the government?"

"Better than you do, in any case! I *am* part of that world, you know!"

"Whoa, okay, then! Let's stop right there. Seriously, I'd like to understand. What's your name? If you want me to introduce you to the others, I'm going to have to tell them who you are."

"I can do that very well all by myself, thank you."

"Well, okay…"

He stands up. He's over six feet tall. He is well-built, with wide shoulders and a broad back. He seems to be in excellent shape, as if he ran for miles with a canoe on his shoulders. He resembles those people – our ancestors – who witnessed the millennia. They were athletes; they lived a very, very old way of life, so old that it can only be remembered by looking at photographs.

The Innu went over to the entrance. Using his hand, he pushed aside the blanket that served as a door. He took a quick look outside.

"We don't have names in today's world," I say. "Well, we have a first name, but after that, it's just numbers. I'm called Kani-89245."

"Kani? That sounds Innu."

"You think so?"

"Yes. My name is Kanukateu. It means 'he has long legs.' I'm too tall for the others!" he laughs.

I start to laugh with him.

"So, it's Kani?"

"Okay, yes, Kani."

"So now then, Kani, how are you feeling?"

"Better, really. It seems like the tea worked."

"Awesome. I'm glad."

I still feel like laughing. Kanukateu speaks with the accent of people I knew during my childhood, over 30 years ago now. It feels good to hear it again.

Since I cannot get up and walk, he stays to keep me company and pour me tea. He prepares some bread on the little stove, and he takes out some red, purple, and orange berries. He makes me a plate with a little jam on the side. There's also an old-fashioned knife. It somehow feels as if I'm back with my *mushum*.

Kanukateu sits near me; he had made a similar plate for himself. He laughs easily, which I like. He has started the fire in a metal oven whose chimney goes up through the roof. It heats the house, which has only one room.

Kanukateu has been assigned to take care of me until I feel better. He tells me that they moved the clan's elders to a separate house to protect them from any disease I might be carrying. Only Kanukateu is allowed to see me for the moment. Once I'm up and about, a doctor from the clan will examine me, and when everything is alright, I'll finally be allowed to move around the village.

He tells me that upon the arrival of the First-to-Come, two of their grandparents were stricken with a skin disease that had originated in one of the Innu cities they'd come from. It was caused by the water they drank because the waste buried by former aluminium operations had contaminated the area's rivers. The erosion of riverbeds had uncovered these buried caches, which had then affected a portion of the population. Some other First-to-Comes were in turn afflicted, and 12 of the 40 who had arrived together died as a result of the illness, which caused extreme dryness of the skin and left horrific scabs. They were buried in the back country Nutshimit, they called it and the village's inhabitants sometimes made pilgrimages there to honour their courage and their lives, as well as their Crossing.

Kanukateu explains that this is the word they use to describe the moment when the men or women known as First-to-Comes were able to pass from one world to another. These people reached the other side because they had knowledge from ancient times that enabled them to do so. He explains to me that this other side is invisible to human beings (and even less visible to artificial life forms because they lack the gift of environmental awareness) and that our earliest ancestors once used this invisible membrane to protect themselves from the dangers of civilization.

"But I thought that because there're no longer great expanses of organic nature, we couldn't use this membrane anymore."

"Yes, but ever since there's been snow everywhere, the ancestors' successors have been able to awaken the pathways to the other side."

Then he told me about the gift of telepathy, which his people commonly use.

"We don't have it anymore! We're not even allowed to use it! It was prohibited by the government of Kanatabe! They were afraid that it would replace technology. It's one of the few human abilities that is categorically forbidden."

"What? C'mon! It should be forbidden to forbid it! It's a human being's inherent right, in my opinion."

"But you know it was always something feared... Do you remember? It was even lost for 200 years!"

"Do I remember? Have you already forgotten that I've lived here since I was born? I haven't seen the world from the other side. I was sure that humans were completely different from us, more evolved, or something like that."

"More evolved?!"

In fact, in the decades that followed the election of Louis Wapstan, first Chief Minister of Kanatabe, he had decided to appoint to serve with him four Prime Ministers of Kanatabe, all Indigenous women and elders who represented nations from all across the country. Telepathy was restored to all the nations. But the non-Indigenous, who had always believed that telepathy had only ever existed in science- fiction stories, had never really trusted those men and women who had the gift. And so it happened that 30 years later, pressure from the population led to the establishment of an advanced technology for communication between humans in an effort to eradicate the nations' use of telepathy. Telepathy was then banned everywhere in Kanatabe, although it was sometimes used illegally. Infrared detection devices were installed in the country's surveillance cameras, and thanks to their hypersensitivity to atoms, it became possible to detect a telepathic exchange between two people.

The thought of being able to use telepathy to communicate is therefore practically taboo for me. But it's also terribly exciting!

"Would you be able to teach me?"

He laughed again. "First tell me about your world, I'd like to know your story. Truth be told, no one has ever left this place since the First-to-Comes arrived. So we know almost nothing about it."

I figure that, at the time the First-to-Comes passed through the invisible membrane, what was then Canada had been experiencing inequalities in its legislation ever since Justin Trudeau had led a coup d'état to remain in power. That had led to unprecedented chaos across the country whereas up until then, from Macdonald to Harper, Canada had had a fairly calm political and social life, despite the great injustices experienced by the First Peoples. Trudeau made so many promises that he managed to calm the fervour somewhat, but the grievances started up again with renewed vigour when the First Peoples realized that after a first, four-year mandate, he had done almost nothing to improve the living conditions in Indigenous communities, which were still known as "reserves" back then. It was an ugly time in our history, and one that had lasted 75 years.

Although Canada was a peaceful nation at that time, in First Peoples' and in their allies' communities, people raged against the indecency with which they were treated. When Trudeau thought he would truly lose the complete confidence of his allies in the House of Commons, he hurriedly and without prior warning signed a decree that immediately adopted the articles of the United Nations Declaration on the Rights of Indigenous Peoples. It created unprecedented tensions not only within his own party but also in Parliament. That was in 2025.

Although this elicited instant and fully warranted joy among First Peoples, the communities weren't ready for such a decree, which had been imposed from one day to the next. Since most of them were accustomed to this kind of sudden political shift under Trudeau's governance, many of them still worked diligently to adapt their policies to that end, to establish a judicial structure with the help of a hoard of Indigenous and non-Indigenous lawyers from all across the country in order to correct the shortcomings of the past and ensure respect for the new constitutional legislation.

Keb developed its own identity much later. What was then Quebec was still a people that couldn't reconcile its past, present and future; and in the labyrinth of their sub-conscious searching, some, having no nation to claim as their own, had decided to try to go for the easy money and to instigate disorder wherever history had left its mark of disillusionment. Wounded by Canada's atrocious record in its treatment of them, the First Peoples no longer knew where to place the boundaries around their hearts, which had been broken by all and sundry.

For this reason, in the years that followed, the Never More movement had solidified the conversation about Indigenous identity. The Canadian Constitution had passed laws and regulations to protect the nations, and the nations each drafted their own Charter of National Identity and Membership. Not only did we have to start protecting our identity from other modern forms of pillage, theft, appropriation, and usurpation, but these tough actions inspired the people to return to their ancestral lands. Never More became a global movement for the reoccupation of Indigenous territory.

"Kani…"

"Yes?"

"You sound like you've been there."

"Ha-ha, I know! I'm very keen on that movement! That's how we were able to redraw the map of the country and rename it Kanatabe. The nations took back their land. I could tell you more about it, but it's super-long. I studied this part of history in detail. The Indigenous now make up 25 per cent of Kanatabe's population, you know, and 37 per cent of Keb's."

"Kani…"

"Yes?"

"You know so many things. You're obviously a very smart person. I admire your strength. Your allegiance to your country has clear, well-defined foundations. You're a warrior for your… Your clan… And then there's my clan. How did you manage to get here? What did you do to pass through the membrane?"

"I learned how from a book."

"What? Which book?"

"A book!"

"A book, how?!"

Kanukateu stood and raised his voice. He was scaring me.

"Don't worry, it wasn't a digital book! It was an actual physical book that I found in the far reaches of Kanatabe's national library…"

"A national library?!"

"Yes, it's huge, enormous, you can get lost in it! There are zillions of e-books now, no one cares about physical books, especially if they're too old."

"You mean to say that there is a physical book that talks about us… do you have it with you?"

My silence gives me away.

"You left it there?!"

Kanukateu sits down on the ground, in front of me. He is panicking.

"That means that others will be coming."

MINISHTIKOK (THE ISLAND)

JANIS OTTAWA

Miko dug at the source to get drinking water, spending hours at it, all of them in vain. Atcak arrived just in time; he implanted the rod and the pipe in the ground. Drawing water from the lake was out of the question. It had been a long time since Miko had only to turn on a tap to get good, clean water... Thoughts of his past life made him momentarily forget his duties as man of the house.

A young girl from the community noticed Miko and threw a tiny rock behind his head. He worked to fill his bucket and quickly stood before she caught up with him. "Boy, can she ever be annoying!" he thought. He approached his camp. His mother, Anas, reminded her only son that he shouldn't waste time. "Time is short!" she'd always say. He poured some water into the pot to heat it for the laundry and the dishes. Anas then sent him to help the men dig the immense pit because winter would be hard that year, and a great many would have to live there. Miko frowned at the idea that he'd have to stay in that place near Anocka and other members of the community, who butted into other people's business.

There was work to be done. It was hardly the time to relax and stare at the sky. Miko looked at his arms, his darkened skin, and the blazing sun. He would have preferred being a different colour, having paler skin, becoming someone else. Then he pulled himself together. This sudden desire to change skin was practically a betrayal of his bloodline as a son of his community's medicine-men. Miko headed over to the pit and heard Akot behind the bushes. Akot was collecting the bark of the *wikwasatikw*, the silver birch, making sure to preserve the tree's various layers, the phloem. He hummed a special chant for each layer, thanking the Creator for the life of this tree. His chant became a prayer; he hoped to be the next one to leave *minishtikok*, the island, to go get provisions in Otenak.

"Akot! Get lots of birch because I'll be the next one to leave *minishtikok*!"

"Keep dreaming! I'll be the one leaving this place."

❦

Anas was having stomach pains. She felt weak. For several mornings now, she had been staying longer in bed. She appealed to *Kitchi Manitou*, imploring the Creator to help her find the plant she sought on *minishtikok*. A good tea, a handful of tobacco in a piece of cloth, and a piece of *pakwecikan* in a canvas bag should help her feel better. It would take time to find what she needed in the forest. The trees seemed to welcome her with open arms, a feeling of comfort filled her heart, and she continued walking, a long branch in her hand. She pushed aside the bushes and carefully examined the leaves on the ground. The sun announced that it would very soon be night. Anas had gone a little too far from the camp, so she prepared a place to rest under a *minihikw*, a white spruce.

><>><<

The young people, the *awacak*, ran through the woods to the hut of *Kokom*, Grandmother, where she was sharing her knowledge. *Moshom* was with her for the day. *Awacak* would learn to imitate *awesisak*, the game animal, to help with the hunt on *minishtikok*. Game was somewhat scarce, and they had to find a way to catch its attention. Miko pressured the hut's supervisor to allow him to listen to the lesson. He looked at the ground as he explained that his late father had not been able to show him how to do this because his father had been killed by *ka wapisitcik*, by White men. Then he hurried to the *shapitowan*, the tent. *Moshom* began teaching and explained that the hunt for big game took place in autumn.

"First, we'll learn the *kotosowan*, the way our ancestors did it, the way they called the moose just in time for the hunt. This way we can make it through the winter," said *Moshom*.

Miko listened to his instructor's chant and got lost in his dreams; he thought of the one who made his heart beat faster. She had hair the colour of flames and eyes as blue as a summer sky. He would do anything to see her again.

><>><<

Miko went back to join Akot and called out to him.

"Akot! Today I'm going to help you collect birchbark because I have a big project. We're going to build a canoe!"

"What are you going to do with it? We can't even leave *minishtikok*. You realize you're risking your life if you leave the island?"

Miko insisted; he would do anything to reach his girl-friend.

"I know! But we'll have enough birch to conceal the colour of my skin and to make the canoe! I have to see her again! I want to go find her, I'm still in love with her, and I'm absolutely certain that she's waiting for me."

"You know that your project has to be approved by the Council of Elders?"

"Yes, and I'm sure they'll turn me down, which is why you have to help me."

"You should first apply for the autumn mission."

Several men had never returned from the mission. What had happened? Had they been killed? Had they suffered before dying? Miko felt his anger rise up inside as he thought about his *otawi*, his father. What had happened to him? Had he abandoned them? What had happened to the provisions and equipment?

Miko assumed that these men had found themselves a charming non-native wife and were living happily with their children in a beautiful house. He had always dreamt of a reconciliation between native and non-native peoples. He was only four years old when he first met the girl with the flame-coloured hair, and she still occupied his thoughts. He had every intention of being the chosen one, of going to see her, of bringing her back to *minishtikok*, and more importantly, of bringing back provisions for the people of his community.

The one who brought enough back was considered to be courageous and earned the community's respect. Miko badly wanted to become that man because the one who was brave was the one who made decisions during meetings and could even be named Chief.

>̃ṽ≺

The time had come to build a shelter to avoid being detected by the air route. The hole was almost finished, the men prepared the materials, and one of them thought that they wouldn't have enough screws or nails. The camp leader suggested first gathering spruce roots, then solidifying the shelter when they had more screws and nails. The committee hurried to gather what they needed, and everyone set to work.

>̃ṽ≺

Miko asked his mother to sit for a moment and answer his questions. She gave him an embarrassed look.

"Tell me what happened in that hospital. I know that they did something bad to our brothers and sisters, and that several of them died. I don't understand! Why did so many die in 2049, what did they do?"

Anas sat, took a deep breath, and began: "Many of us were killed in the hospitals. Those who developed cancer were left to fend for themselves or were helped to speed their departure to the spirit world of our ancestors. Our chiefs also fought to save our lands, and we were defeated. Pipelines were laid from one end of the country to the other. Wherever pipelines can be seen, there used to be Indigenous communities, but today they're all gone, everyone is dead. The new government had promised assistance for low-income Indigenous families and was supposed to bring food to several communities. The families were poisoned, and then the investigators reported mass suicides. Meanwhile, our people learned that a number of communities had been decimated. *Okimaw*, the chief, ordered us to refuse anything coming from the outside world, and we came to take refuge here. I still wonder what the future has in store for us. I ask myself many questions – if, for example, other nations still live on the territory… Your father agreed to be the chosen one because he always believed that life had returned to normal in Otenak and that reconciliation with the other peoples had been finalized. He never returned, and so, my son, I'm telling you not to go, I don't want to suffer again, I could not bear it."

Outside, a voice drew nearer. It was the chief calling the community together to name the chosen one.

Miko responded in a firm tone: "I want to know what is going on in the city, I'm sure that we can go back and live in the house. It makes no sense to me to think that we couldn't live together on our own territory. Something must be done, but for now, I'm preparing to be the chosen one. I plan to protect myself and carefully camouflage the colour of my skin."

He left to find his friend Akot so they could continue gathering *wikwasatikw*. The second of the uppermost layers of *wikwas* was heated in bear grease to make the paste used to prepare the chosen one, the most difficult part being the covering of his face. Several of the chosen had learned at that point that they were allergic to birchbark. Marty was chosen, and Miko hoped he would have an allergic reaction because he was the second to be chosen.

Miko felt himself growing angry; he felt as if he was being held prisoner on *minishtikok*. Exploring life away from the island was his only option, and he firmly intended to leave and go see for himself if his sweetheart still thought of him, if she was still waiting for him. "I don't want to be an Anishinaabe anymore," he said to himself. And then he regretted it: "It's crazy to want to change your identity, you might as well die." His memories rose to the surface. She had eyes as blue as the sky, and she was always in his thoughts…

UAPUCH-UNAIKAN

Alyssa Jérôme

"I need to get close to nature. I want to feel my body wedded to our Nitassinan, its moss and its humid soil, especially its beautiful territories in the north. The place where I am at home. I haven't been there yet, but I feel that a part of me is already there. The dry needles at the base of the fir trees, the twigs and small rocks mean little to me. They are nothing compared to the invisible suffering that the city forces me to endure. I want the sunbathing in its blue sky to blind me to all that I've seen up until now. I want to breathe fresh air fragrant with the majestic woodlands that rise from the rich soil. My ears need relief; I need to hear the birds singing their beguiling serenades in the forest. And I... I need to be distracted by little branches that snap and crackle when animals pass, to be lulled by the gentle, treasured sound of rivers that once guided my brave ancestors. I want to gather my own fruits, the ones that taste so sour but so very real. I dream of tracking my own game, the animal that I would respect, for which I would be grateful, and which would cause me to say a thousand thank yous. I yearn to know a better life."

Anahite was one of today's rare dreamers. Every morning, before leaving her bright, modern apartment, she took the time to activate the mirror next to the front door to see herself smile. She tried to convince herself that she could change the world this very day, even if it was already doomed, too automated, too far from human…

Then as she did every morning, she went out, feeling self-defeated, staring at the perfectly clean metallic floor in which she could study her own reflection. As always, her smile disappeared behind her black hair. She looked at herself for a few more seconds, until she began to feel that someone was watching. Out of the corner of her eye, she thought she caught the silhouette of a willowy woman and a four-legged animal. She immediately raised her head but saw nothing more. She peered down the two empty hallways that led to her door and told herself that no one could get away that quickly. She closed her eyes, then let her mind reassure her… it was only an illusion. After opening her eyes again, Anahite put her earbuds in, played a song on her telephone, and then took the day's first steps outside her home, sliding the tips of her long, thin fingers along the corridor's white wall.

It was a very special day for Anahite. She had spent the last 10 years teaching her nation's basic principles to the children of the White Elite. She had shared all her knowledge with the biggest of smiles and in the most pleasant mood of anyone in District 31. She had been promised a comfortable retirement, and she breathed happiness as she walked. She could already feel nature.

The government had offered to make a pact with the First Nations, as it had so often done, but this time, it was not a question of money, and what it was asking for in return had nothing to do with territory. "Share your knowledge with our children for 10 years, and then each one of you will have the right to live as you once did – free, on your own land."

With her head down, she gazed at herself as she walked the entire length of the corridor. So proud of herself, so accomplished – she wanted to look at the floor, which had reflected her image as she went to school each day. This was the last time. She observed her dark, slanted eyes, which glanced rapidly down her elongated nose to her well-defined lips. She noticed her big, pink cheeks. She was proud to be Innu and to have been so resilient!

When she arrived at the school's door, a tall man with curly hair was blocking the way.

"What are you doing here? You have no right to enter."

"Hi! I've been teaching here for 10 years as of today… I came to get the pension I was promised!"

"Promise of a pension? That's a laugh! You're all the same and always have been, so easy to fool… There was never any pension! Get outta here, or I'll take care of you myself."

Anahite's heart began to pound. She didn't understand anything anymore. Suddenly, a sharp sound struck her ears. The man, seeing that the young woman wasn't leaving, pushed her. She fell to the ground. At that very moment, Anahite thought she was receiving the only thing she deserved: contempt for having spent her whole life believing her government's lies. The pain she felt was the pain of her body being torn from her soul. She closed her eyes.

Crumpled over, Anahite felt as if she were falling through emptiness while malicious hands kept trying to touch her. She wished her mother were there. She remembered those rare times when her mother would come up behind her and take her in her arms, singing lullabies. She imagined arms embracing her and tried to feel their strength and their warmth. She wanted her memories to be more powerful than her sorrows, but each day made them fade. She needed her mother. Her mother was her hero, a woman of such strong character, a warrior. But in thrall to her weaknesses and fears, Anahite had lost her family. She was the very opposite of her mother, who would surely be ashamed of her. Her mother was always ready and willing to defend her people. Today, she was undoubtedly busy, peacefully gathering berries.

～⌒〜⌒〜

Anahite opened her eyes. She would have been happy to find that this was just a nightmare, but she realized that she was in a different place, far from District 31. Everything seemed older there, and abandoned. The air wasn't filtered, unlike in her district where everything was modern and regulated. She was lying on a wet tile floor, and the room was filled with the strong odour of cheap cigarettes. A palpable tension gripped the little condo, which was scarcely lit by the brownish bulb in the stove's hood. Anahite was again overcome by fear. She had never left the district since the day she was born. Never would she have imagined that her first outing would be to such an unexceptional sector.

Suddenly, she felt a warm hand come to rest on her shoulder. A shiver ran through her, but then the hand gently pushed her hair aside to uncover her face. Curious, Anahite raised her eyes and saw a beautiful, dark-skinned woman whose face glowed with youth. She had shiny dark hair and a radiant smile. She raised Anahite's chin to examine her more closely.

"Oh, sweetheart, come with me, I'll draw you a bath, we'll get you back on your feet! I'm here, don't worry…"

The woman used a washcloth to pour water over Anahite. The falling water echoed terribly in the little bathroom, but she found every drop that ran over her body deeply reassuring.

"My name is Niki. What's yours, love?"

"Anahite."

"Oh, wow, I really like your name! Are you Indigenous?"

"Yes…"

"I never would have guessed! You're too pretty for that! Want a cigarette?"

"No, thanks, I don't smoke."

"You don't smoke or you've never tried? Watch how I do it…"

Niki lit the end of her thin cigarette and brought it to her full lips, gently inhaling. She closed her eyes as she blew the smoke toward the ceiling. She began to laugh and then handed the cigarette to Anahite.

"No need to feel embarrassed around me, girl." Amazed by her confidence, Anahite took a puff.

"That looks good on you, it makes you look really badass!"

Anahite's heart was beating fast. Not from fear this time, but from joy. She felt strangely good around Niki. Niki put her at ease. She hadn't felt that since her mother retired. Niki was definitely a special woman.

"You shouldn't be here, love, it's not healthy, and you deserve better…"

"Do you know how I can get out of here?"

"Yes… I'd really like to help you, but I can't, I have to respect my man."

"He's your man?"

"Not by choice… Listen, there's some money in the kitchen cupboard, above the sink…"

"I'll never be able to! I'm so, so weak…"

"Oh, sweetie, take my pack of cigarettes. Every time you believe you're weak, smoke one! It'll pick you right up, just like this nice bath did!"

The sentence reminded her of her mother. Any time she saw that Anahite was in a bad mood, she would wrap her in her arms and invite her to perform a little ceremony. There had been smoke to cleanse whatever negative things she might have seen, heard or touched. Anahite would take some tobacco in her left hand and evince happiness for her mother, her family, her inner circle and obviously for herself. It had done her a world of good. But she had stopped. As if her identity had been disappearing over the course of the days spent alone in her apartment, without family or friends, because the government had promised them all a retirement worthy of the name.

Suddenly the front door opened with a bang. A deep voice could be heard in the condo.

"Niki! Where's the girl I brought back?"

Niki gave Anahite a towel and a red satin bathrobe and then went to join the man. Anahite took a deep breath and began to embody her thoughts: "I am strong, I am capable, I am lucky, I am grabbing this chance to escape, I am strong."

Then she too left the bathroom and looked toward the back door, near which Niki and the man were now standing. Her eyes met the man's. She opened the front door located right next to the bathroom and began to run.

She wheezed and breathing hurt. Her eyes watered; her heart was pounding faster than her feet. In a stroke of bad luck, she became trapped on an old viaduct. Men came from every direction. She backed up and roughly collided with a cold metal surface. She was startled and glanced behind her. A noisy brown river was running below. She had but one thing to do: jump for dear life.

She turned and began to climb over the guardrail, but a man caught her. With a smile on his lips, he pinned her to the ground, suffocating her under his weight. He kept her from moving by restraining her wrists.

"Calm down, little one. Us guys, we need you."

Anahite was undaunted; she managed to knee the man between the legs, and he howled in pain. The young woman rolled over, slipped through the viaduct's rungs, and fell into the river.

⤕⤖

Before anything else, Anahite smelled the ground she'd fallen on – soft, warm, wet ground. Then she heard leaves in the wind, noises made by animals. She detected the scent of pine and the freshness of a river. She opened her eyes, and a brilliant sun blinded her. She couldn't believe it. Was she really in the natural world? In the wilderness she's always dreamed of? She tried to get up but failed. She was in too much pain. Her mad dash and dive had exhausted her. All of a sudden, she noticed an animal watching her closely. She felt that she was being watched the same way she'd been watched earlier in the day, but this time is was real. The animal had a delicate reddish fur and a black line down its back. It walked softly around the young woman, with an inquisitive air. Its paws did a strange little dance backward and then forward, as if vacillating between returning to woods and approaching Anahite. It was the first time that Anahite was seeing a wild animal. And the first one she was meeting was her beloved mother's favourite, a sly one.

She had no idea how to react. She'd always been told to remain calm because such animals were not accustomed to seeing humans. But this fox was unafraid. It seemed to want to come closer. In any case, Anahite knew that the animal had no intention of harming her. So she went down on all fours and approached the animal with kindness. But the closer she got, the stronger her impression that she knew this fox. Had it appeared in her dreams? Suddenly and without warning, it darted off. A strong wind choked the young woman. A helicopter was descending directly overhead. She tried to follow the fox, but it had already disappeared.

"Anahite! Don't go any further! I'm here to make sure you get the retirement you were expecting!"

She stopped and went over to the helicopter, which had landed on a rock. She recognized the pilot as the man who had been talking to Niki, back at the apartment she'd escaped. He exited the helicopter and walked toward her. He offered her his hand, a big smile on his face.

"Follow me, and we'll settle all this in the city!"

"I don't want to go back to the city! I was promised a life in the forest, and now I'm here! I want to stay here!"

"Don't you worry, you'll be back in no time!"

Anahite was trembling; she no longer trusted anyone… She didn't know what to think anymore.

"Why wasn't I told earlier that this retirement was nothing but a sham?"

"A profiteer preying on beautiful young women! For that, I am truly sorry."

She noticed the fox lurking in the woods nearby. It appeared to be signalling her to follow. The two stared at each other for a brief moment. Suddenly, Anahite realized that the animal had one blue eye and one brown eye. Just like her mother.

In that instant, she understood the atrocity of history. Anahite shouted her mother's name and started to run toward the animal. The man took off in hot pursuit.

The young woman used all her strength to reach the forest. CRACK! A horrible sound echoed through the woods. The birds shrieked and took wing. Anahite fell; she'd been shot in the leg. She was crying, suffering. The man drew near.

"Ah, my lovely Anahite… you are one of today's rare dreamers. That makes you dangerous. You spread false ideas among normal people. You are the cause of all the problems in the world."

"Me? Look what you've done! You've… turned the members of my nation into… into animals!"

"You wanted us to help you save the flora and fauna? Well, there you go!"

"That's disgusting."

"Why? You want to be treated like savages! This time, we're respecting your true nature. In the end, we're all winners here! C'mon, it's time to give you a makeover, my little bunny rabbit…"

UATAN,
A BEATING HEART

Joséphine Bacon

A starry night and me.
I think I'm hearing footsteps.
An old man, caribou antlers about his waist,
    white jacket embroidered with red, pierces the horizon.
Grandfather, I no longer hear your heart.
I know.

Who is this man? Does he come from space? Has he returned from the past? What is his connection to the animals? Why is a pattern of antlers embroidered on his jacket? Napessiss awakens in Nutshimit, in the village of Uatan, in the year 2070, troubled by his dream.

Ever since the Innu left the coast and returned to their ancestral lands to rediscover their roots, few men go hunting. More focus is placed on the cultivation of plants, vegetables, and fruit in the vast greenhouses that feed the community, while animals are left in peace. Napessiss knows that his father remembers the wisdom of the elders. He sometimes sees his father leaving to go north and returning with a lake trout whose bones he separates from the head, without understanding why. His father, a secretive and silent man, never told him about their ancestors.

This morning, for the first time, Napessiss accompanies his father into the taiga.

"How did the hunters dress back in the day?"

His father signals to him to be quiet.

The joy that Napessiss felt at sharing his dream disappeared, giving way to sadness.

On the shores of Lac Kukames, he imitates his father's actions.

Hours pass to the sound of lines cast into the calm water.

A lake trout takes the bait on Napessiss' hook.

With a proud smile on his face, his father teaches him how to clean the fish.

He tells him to put the fish guts back in the water.

"Everything we do has meaning. When you return to the water the parts of the fish that we won't eat, you're showing a sign of respect to the Master of Aquatic Animals. The same is true when the women made a hunter's clothing; they showed their respect for the Master of the Caribou. They take great care when they paint the white leather from which they sew the hunter's jacket. Tshishikushkueu, the woman from space who watches over the Earth, loves beauty. The women hoped that their needlework would please Tshishikushkueu so that she would notice their husband and lead him to the caribou. My grandfather wore a jacket decorated with ochre."

"Did his jacket have a pattern of caribou antlers on it?

"Why do you ask?"

"Last night, I dreamt..."

Napessiss goes to bed, pleased to have shared the day with his father. His eyes come to rest on the drum hanging on the wall of his room. This *teueikan* belonged to his great-grandfather.

A heart beats.

The beating awakens him with a start.
Was it the sound of his drum?
He falls back to sleep.

A woman embroiders a garment for the drum.
Antlers, flowers, canoes. She stitches and stitches on the cloth that she's making for the drum.

This time, he won't wait to speak of his dream. As soon as he is awake, he tells his father about it.

"I did tell you, my son, that a drum is sacred. It can't be turned into a decorative object. There *is* a garment for your drum. Ask your mother. She will know."

Napessiss delicately takes the drum off the wall and respectfully clothes it.

All drum players must have had three dreams about the *teueikan* before they can make use of it.

At the age of 14, Napessiss had heard footsteps, then a heart beating. He had seen a woman's hands protecting the drum. His dreams return to Uatan the spark of an almost-forgotten past.

THE AUTHORS

Marie-Andrée Gill is Pekuakamishkueu. Poet, author, host of decolonizing podcasts (*Laissez-nous raconteur : l'histoire crochie, Les Mots de Joséphine*), and contributor to the radio show *Plus on est de fous, plus on lit*, she is also a PhD candidate at the Université du Québec in Chicoutimi. Her Master's thesis dealt with decolonization through personal writing. She has published three volumes of poetry *Béante*, *Frayer*, and *Chauffer le dehors* and has contributed to numerous collections. For her work and her artistic outlook, Gill was named artist of the year in Saguenay–Lac-Saint-Jean (CALQ) in 2020.

Katia Bacon is an Innu from Pessamit. At the age of five, her cousin taught her to read, and she has been passionate about reading ever since. *Cécile* is her first short story, as well as the first name of her grandmother, with whom Katia has lived since moving to Montreal in 2015.

Louis-Karl Picard-Sioui, originally from Wendake, is a historian, anthropologist, writer, poet, and visual arts curator. He prefers not to be categorized, defining himself first and foremost as a creator. His poetry has appeared in periodicals, exhibitions and on the Internet. It has been recited in Canada and abroad, published together in four volumes, included in a number of collections, and even adapted for an animated film.

Virginia Pésémapéo Bordeleau was born in Jamésie, in northwestern Quebec. She is a multi-disciplinary Cree artist. In 2006, she won the excellence in creation award from the Conseil des arts et des lettres du Québec and the Télé-Québec distinction in poetry. In 2012, she won the Prix littéraire de l'Abitibi-Témiscamingue. Since 2007, she has published three novels, three poetry collections, a storybook, an essay, and an art book. In 2020, she was chosen Abitibi-Témiscamingue's artist of the year by the Conseil des arts et lettres du Québec and presented a 40-year retrospective at Rouyn-Noranda's art museum.

Michel Jean is an Innu writer and journalist from the Mashteuiatsh community. He has published nine books, including seven novels, and directed two short story collections (*Amun* and *Wapke*). His novel, *Kukum*, won the Prix littéraire France-Québec 2020 and the VLEEL prize in 2021.

Jean Sioui has published two novels for young adults, *Hannenorak* and *Hannenorak et le vent*, with publisher Loup de Gouttière. He has also published seven volumes of poetry: *Le Pas de l'Indien* et *Poèmes rouges*, *L'avenir voit rouge* and *Entre moi et l'arbre*, for which he was selected as a finalist for the Académie des lettres du Québec's Prix Alain-Grandbois (poetry), *Je suis île*, *Avant le gel des visages*, and *Mon couteau croche*. A member of the Wendat nation, he writes in the spirit of First Nations culture, that of his ancestors and thus his own through inheritance is a source for his writings. His work is motivated by his involvement with budding Aboriginal authors and by his participation in numerous artistic events. He strongly supports principles of respect, integrity, and social justice, as well as an approach that promotes the preservation of Huron-Wendat heritage and culture. Steeped in these values, he follows in the Indian's footsteps.

Cyndy Wylde is Anishinaabe and Atikamekw from the Pikogan community, located in northeastern Abitibi-Témiscamingue. Marked by the consequences of colonization and sedentation on her family, she was very young when she decided that she wanted to rectify the effects that assimilation policies have had on all First Nations. After 25 years spent working for the federal correctional services, she became a PhD candidate in the École d'études Indigenous at the Université du Québec en Abitibi-Témiscamingue (UQAT) and shifted her research to focus on custodial over-representation of Quebec's First Nations women. She was a member of the research team at the Public Inquiry Commission on relations between Indigenous Peoples and certain public services in Québec: listening, reconciliation and progress. She is a policy advisor for the Assemblée des First Nations Québec-Labrador (APNQL). She is also a consultant for several Indigenous organizations and a lecturer at various universities. Her unusual career path has proved to be a strength and catalyst for educating people whenever possible.

Elisapie Isaac was born in Salluit, Nunavik. After studying communications, she directed a documentary dedicated to her adoptive grandfather, earning her the prize for best young director at the Rendez-vous du cinema québécois in 2004. She also became known as writer-composer-performer as part of the duo Taïma, which won a Juno Award in 2005. In 2010 she put out her first solo album, on which she sang in Inuktitut, French, and English. Very much taken with the work of Félix Leclerc and the poetry of Richard Desjardins, she has made her mark as a strong and very popular Inuk voice.

Isabelle Picard is an advisor on Indigenous affairs at Radio-Canada. She was a columnist for the series, *Kebec*, at Télé-Québec and a contributor to *La Presse+*. An ethnologist, she is a lecturer at UQAM and is part of CIÉRA (Centre interuniversitaire d'études et de recherches autochtones). She is also a writer. Her first young adult novel, *Nish, tome 1 – Le nord et le sud*, was published by Les Malins in April 2021.

J.D. Kurtness was born in Chicoutimi to a French-Canadian mother and an Innu father from Mashteuiatsh. She moved to Montreal with a plan to study microbes, but ended up dedicated to writing and, more recently, to computer science. Her first novel, *De vengeance*, was published by L'instant même in 2017. Both "noir" and humorous, the book quickly received positive reviews from critics. Her second novel, *Aquariums*, a work of science fiction in which humanity falls victim to an unprecedented epidemic, was published in 2019. She now intends to write about peace in the world.

Natasha Kanapé Fontaine is a poet, author, actor, and interdisciplinary artiste from the Innu community of Pessamit, on the North Shore. Mémoire d'encrier has published her works, *N'entre pas dans mon âme avec tes chaussures* (Poetry prize from the Société des Écrivains francophones d'Amérique 2013), *Manifeste Assi* (2014), and *Bleuets et abricots* (2016). *Kuei, je te salue* (Écosociété, 2016), written as a conversation with Deni Ellis Béchard, is the "place to find words that create an opening" for the people and for future generations, deconstructing racism between Quebec's Native and non-Native peoples. It has been translated into English as is *Kuei, My Friend*. Québec Amérique has also published her short story *"Sky dancer"* in *Les Disparus d'Ély – Mortels*.

Janis Ottawa is an Atikamekw mother and *kukom* from Manawan. A teacher by profession, she teaches in her maternal language at the elementary school level. A nomad at heart, she travels by air, by road, by river, and by reading, too. An actor in her spare time, she played a major role in Chloé Leriche's 2016 film, *Avant les rues*, a role she performed in the Atikamekw language. Janis is a proud ambassador for her language and culture, sharing her passion through traditional dance at pow-wows and through her magnificent beadworks.

Alyssa Jérôme, born in 1998, is an emerging Métis multidisciplinary artist from the Innu community of Uashat Mak Mani-Utenam. At just 15 years old, she published her first young adult novel, *Le Rêve éveillé de Salma*. Two years later, she published its sequel, *Le Rêve éveillé d'Amethyst*.

Joséphine Bacon is a poet, lyricist and filmmaker. In 2010, her collection, *Bâtons à message / Tshissinuatshitakana* received the Marché de la poésie de Montréal's Prix des lecteurs. Published in 2013, *Un thé dans la toundra / Nipishapui nete mushuat* was a finalist for Canada's Governor General's Award and for the Grand Prix du livre de Montréal. In 2019, she won the Prix des libraires, in the Quebec poetry category, for her collection *Uiesh / Quelque part*. One of Quebec's leading authors, Joséphine Bacon has received numerous honours, including an honorary doctorate from the Université Laval in 2016. In 2018, she was named a member of the Ordre des arts et des lettres du Québec and an officer of the Ordre de Montréal. She has taught Innu-aimun for over 40 years and gives many writing workshops and lectures in universities, CEGEPs, and a number of Indigenous communities.

TRANSLATOR'S NOTES

(SCAN THE QRs FOR RELATED ONLINE RESOURSES / URLs PAGE 159)

TEN DAYS ON BIRCHBARK

The Cree words for grandma and grandpa are *kukum* and *mushum*. There are a variety of spellings (kokum, kôhkom, kokom, moshom, etc. Here, and in the other short stories in this collection, I am using each author's own spelling.

THE TOMAHAWK AND THE SWORD

The Strendu is a mythological stone giant in Huron and Iroquois tribal lore. Its skin is as hard as stone and can repel all normal weapons.

 Literally translated from Wendat, *Ahskennon'nia iye's* means "I am in peace" or "I'm going in peace," but has come to mean "I'm doing well."

Toronto: According to Canadian scholar John Steckley, PhD, the city's name comes from the Mohawk word *tkaronto*, which means "where there are trees in the water" and may date back to native peoples who drove stakes into the water to create fish weirs.

Skawendat is defined as "a single voice" on page 74 of Megan Elizabeth Lukaniec's dissertation, *The elaboration of verbal structure: Wendat (Huron) verb morphology*. 2018. University of California at Santa Barbara.

Stadacona was a 16th Century Iroquois village located near the present-day site of Québec City. Jacques Cartier arrived there in 1535 and wintered nearby.

The mother goddess Yäatayenhtsihk is known as Sky Woman or Ataensic in Huron-Wendat. She is said to have fallen through a hole in the sky.

PAKAN (DIFFERENTLY)

The author spells the Anishinaabemowin greeting "hi" as *k8e* and the word for "muskrat" as *8atcack*. These words have alternative spellings *kuei* and *wazhashk*, respectively that are somewhat easier for a reader to pronounce, so I have used them here.

Forest Alert is the English title of a 1999 documentary by Richard Desjardins and Robert Monderie, which denounced the abusive exploitation and destruction of an environment found nowhere else in the world: Quebec's boreal forest.

KANATABE ISHKUEU

Ishkueu is the Innu-aimun word for woman.

Innuat is the plural of Innu.

MINISHTIKOK (THE ISLAND)

Kice manito is the Anishinaabe creator god and literally means "Great Spirit." It is also spelled Kitchi Manitou. Kitche Manitou (Basil Johnston: *Ojibway Heritage: The ceremonies, rituals, songs, dances, prayers and legends of the Ojibway*. McClelland and Stewart 1976, reprinted 1998; Toronto.), or Gitchi Manitou

Pakwecikan is the Atikamekw word for bannock, a quick flatbread, and literally translates as "to take with the hands."

UAPUCH-UNAIKAN

The title means "rabbit trap."

URLs for QR codes:

THE TOMAHAWK AND THE SWORD

www.native-languages.org/stonecoat.htm

languewendat.com/en/detail/?tag=4-phr-0019

www.theglobeandmail.com/news/national/a-defining-moment-for-tkaronto/article18432992/

www.native-languages.org/wyandot-legends.htm

PAKAN (DIFFERENTLY)

ojibwe.lib.umn.edu/search?utf8=%E2%9C%93&q=muskrat&commit=Search&type=english

KANATABE ISHKUEU

www.noslangues-ourlanguages.gc.ca/en/blogue-blog/innu-langue-en-transformation-rapidly-transforming-language-eng)

MINISHTIKOK (THE ISLAND)

www.thecanadianencyclopedia.ca/en/article/ojibwa

UAPUCH-UNAIKAN

www.pc.gc.ca/en/pn-np/on/pukaskwa/culture/autochtone-indigenous/recit-story

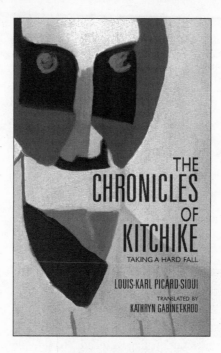

KITCHIKE
TAKING A HARD FALL
LOUIS-KARL PICARD-SIOUI
TRANSLATED BY KATHERYN GABINET-KROO

In his first collection of stories Louis-Karl Picard-Sioui takes us on
a journey into the heart of a very colourful Indigenous community where
traditions, dreams, deprivation and, yes, corruption exist side by side.

With image-laden language, he plunges us into the daily life of
ordinary men and women facing political, economic, and mythical forces
beyond their control. With wry humour and a touch of the fantastic,
the author depicts the sometimes tense relationships in Southern Quebec's
communities, allowing a snapshot of our multicultural society to be seen
between the lines. *The Chronicles of Kitchike* transports us to a unique universe,
to a world that is not only comical but also gentle and replete with legend,
home to a panoply of characters we're not likely to soon forget!

A GATHERING OF INDIGENOUS STORIES SELECTED BY
Michel Jean
TRANSLATED BY
Kathryn Gabinet-Kroo

AMUN
A GATHERING OF INDIGENOUS STORIES
SELECTED BY MICHEL JEAN
TRANSLATED BY KATHERYN GABINET-KROO

In the Innu language, amun means "gathering." Under the direction of
Innu writer and journalist Michel Jean, this collection brings together
Indigenous authors from different backgrounds, First Nations, and generations.
Their works of fiction sometimes reflect history and traditions, other times
the reality of First Nations in Canada. Offering the various perspectives
of well-known creators, this book presents the theatre of a gathering
and the speaking out of people who are too rarely heard.

Authors: Natasha Kanapé Fontaine, Melissa Mollen Dupuis, Louis-Karl Picard-Sioui,
Virginia Pésémapéo Bordeleau, Naomi Fontaine, Alyssa Jérôme, Michel Jean,
Jean Sioui, Maya Cousineau-Mollen, and Joséphine Bacon.

"Ten different stories set in multiple epochs and contexts, offering glimpses
of lives that provide a wider view and understanding of Indigenous experiences."
—*Montreal Review of Books*

BAWAAJIGAN
STORIES OF POWER
CO-EDITED BY NATHAN NIIGAN NOODIN ADLER
AND CHRISTINE MISKONOODINKWE SMITH

Ranging from gritty to gothic, hallucinatory to prophetic, the reader encounters ghosts haunting residential school hallways and ghosts looking on from the after-life, bead-dreamers, talking eagles, Haudenosaunee wizards, giant snakes, sacred white buffalo calves, spider's silk, a burnt and blood-stained diary, wormholes, poppy-induced deliriums, Ouija boards, and imaginary friends among the many exhilarating forces that drive the Indigenous dream-worlds of today.

"This is, overall, a stunning collection of writing from Indigenous sources, stories with the power to transform character and reader alike…the high points are numerous and often dizzying in their force…" —*Quill & Quire*

The Life Crimes and Hard Times of RICKY ATKINSON Leader of the DIRTY TRICKS GANG

A TRUE STORY

RICHARD ATKINSON WITH JOE FIORITO

THE LIFE CRIMES AND HARD TIMES OF RICKY ATKINSON: LEADER OF THE DIRTY TRICKS GANG

RICHARD ATKINSON WITH JOE FIORITO

This is the life story of Ricky Atkinson, who grew up fast and hard in one of Toronto's toughest neighbourhoods during the social ferment of the 1960s, '70s, and '80s. His life was made all the more difficult coming from a black, white, and First Nations mixed family. Under his leadership, the gang eventually robbed more banks and pulled off so many jobs that it is unrivalled in Canadian history. Follow him from the mean streets to backroom plotting, to jail and back again, as he learns the hard lessons of leadership, courage and betrayal.

"Atkinson's memoir is as riveting as true crime gets… It is also a reckoning of the city's racist sins. [and he] makes the convincing connection between societal preju- dice and crime in minority communities. It's a revelatory and fascinating story told from a rare perspective." —Publishers Weekly, starred review

THE SILENCE
KAREN LEE WHITE

In *The Silence*, with the Yukon as a canvas, White engages in a deep empathy
for characters, emergent Indigenous identity, and discovery that employs dreams,
spirits, songs, and journals as foundations for dialogue between cultures, immersing
the reader in a transitional world of embattled ethos and mythos. Her first novel is
a *cri de coeur* that lives alongside Smart's *By Grand Central
Station I Sat Down and Wept* and Kogawa's *Obasan*.

Karen Lee White holds the torch brightly as a new and powerful voice,
her style and sensibility encompassing the traditional and the contemporary.

Includes (on the inside cover) a CD of the author/songwriter/musician's
original music.